WHAT READERS ARE SAYING ABOUT THE TRUE LIES OF REMBRANDT ␣␣␣␣'E:

Easily the best of the series so far! Can't w~

Definitely another thrilling installme␣␣␣␣␣␣␣␣␣␣␣␣␣␣ries and I'm looking forward to the next one. Start␣␣␣␣␣␣␣␣␣␣␣␣ ll be hooked like I am! – *Kelly, Best in Suspense*

My favorite one in the series so far! That may␣␣␣␣ecause I have become so invested in this story line and these characters. – *Nicole*

All I can say is, jump on the DJW train. Best new author I've read in a long time. Thank you, Mr Warren for a few hours of life distraction. I appreciate it. – *Todd*

Rembrandt faces incredibly high stakes, and he battles all sorts of physical challenges, dangers, and threats to save the day. They'll keep you on the edge of your seat – and isn't that, really, the very best place to read? – *Amy*

Just when I think the authors can't turn Rembrandt's life more upside down, they throw in a major TWIST! – *Sarita*

Goodness. I feel like Rembrandt Stone is ruining me for other books. Like, nothing compares to Rem. Seriously, nothing compares. – *Kelly*

There is plenty of action and adrenaline...for how could this book be a Rembrandt Stone book without the chills-racing-down-the-spine suspense? – *MJSH*

It keeps getting better. This whirlpool we seem to have thrust ourselves into that won't let us quit. – *Ochegba*

I got my copy of this book at midnight last night, stayed up until 4 am reading it because I couldn't put it down, and still don't regret it this morning! – *Linda*

Susan May Warren, James L. Rubart and David Curtis Warren are, without a doubt, one of the best groupings I have ever read. – *Jessica*

Once again, I am sitting here, a bit at loss for words. This incredible, crazy, absolutely outstanding, thriller of a series...it continues! – *Rosalyn*

THE TRUE LIES
OF REMBRANDT STONE

CAST THE FIRST STONE

NO UNTURNED STONE

STICKS AND STONE

SET IN STONE

BLOOD FROM A STONE

HEART OF STONE

Set In Stone

TriStone Media Group
Minneapolis, MN

Tristone Media Inc.

15100 Mckenzie Blvd

Minnetonka, Minnesota, 55345

Copyright © 2021 by Tristone Media

ISBN: 978-1-954023-07-9

www.RembrandtStone.com

SOLI DEO GLORIA

CHAPTER 1

What is happiness? Is it a place? A time? A choice?

I am afraid of the answer. Because if it is either of the former two, it's lost to me.

Lost in time, a place that has vanished by my own making and I stand in the wasteland of my choices.

Except, not a wasteland, really. Because I have nearly everything I want.

Nearly.

"Rembrandt, come to bed. It's cold out."

The voice lifts from the beautiful woman under our covers, my wife of seven years, which is almost correct.

Close enough, really, to the truth.

Maybe this *is* my truth.

I'm standing at the open window of my two-story craftsman home. The bare wood floor chills my feet, and a crispness layers the June air, as if the night is on alert.

The sky is a deep indigo, stars staring down at me. The giant dead elm tree at the back of our yard, still here, despite my taking it down in a previous timeline, stretches skeletal arms across the yard and through moonlight waxing my backyard.

In my dreams, I see a swing set there, a little girl, age seven, swinging, her braids flopping with every pump. *Daddy, watch me!*

She is blonde and sweet, and her laughter fills my soul.

My throat burns and I have my answer.

Happiness is a person.

Movement, the bed clothes rustling, then the creak of the floor and I still as Eve comes up and wraps her strong arms around me. She is warm and solid and real and this should be enough for me.

A kiss to my spine sends a ripple of heat through me.

I've missed her so much, my body aches.

"Thinking about your new job?" She smells of the lavender cream she lathers onto her skin every night.

It feels like a lifetime since I've wrapped my hands around hers, since we've shared this quiet awareness of each other.

Three lifetimes, actually.

Because this is my third try at rewriting my life, to find myself back at the beginning.

And like I said, this time, I nearly got it right.

"Yep," I say to her question, lying.

Eve's referring to the job of interim police chief looming ahead of me.

"You've wanted this your entire life," she says. "Even before Booker died."

She comes around and stands in front of me. She's wearing one of my white T-shirts, her legs bare, her kinky auburn hair spiraling out as if she's been shocked. Her green eyes find mine in the darkness, and I'm caught.

This woman loves me.

And that has made all the difference in my life. It anchors me to now, to the fact that *nearly* right is a good place to be.

I put my arms around her and pull Eve to myself. "I hope I can be half the chief Booker was."

"You will be."

I want to ask her what happened after Booker died—not from cancer, or then from an ambush-slash-bombing of a suspect's house, but this time from a robbery-slash-shooting some twenty years ago.

I found out last night, after returning from the past.

Yeah, you heard right.

I am a time traveler.

It almost gives me relief to admit this, because the alternatives are dark and probably involve a long-term placement in a psychiatric clinic.

How I got here, to this now, with Eve in my arms, is a long story, the details tangled and knotted. The short of it is, they involve a watch, bequeathed to me by my former mentor, John Booker, my cold cases, and a daughter my wife doesn't remember, Ashley.

It pains me to think she'll never meet our daughter, even if we should have another child someday, and as I lift her chin, rub my thumb down her cheek, I see a grief in her eyes she probably can't even name.

Maybe somehow, deep in her soul, she knows.

But this is not the end. Someday, we will have an Ashley. I have to believe that.

"I love you, Eve." The words unroll from me easily, words that before might have been less realized.

But traveling through time makes a man sharper. Keener.

Maybe a little bolder, at least when it comes to the uncoiling the emotions deep inside.

She smiles, and I'm a heartbeat from taking her back to our bed when she says, "I should have said yes the first time you asked."

The first time…

She presses her hands onto my chest, sighs. "I keep thinking about the fact that it's probably too late for us. That if we had started sooner, then maybe…" Her eyes are glistening now, and I'm cobbling up the fragments of our history, anything, so I can know how to respond.

Is this because of Burke and Shelby? Because Shelby is pregnant? Shelby is roughly the same age as Eve, so maybe it's not too late, if not risky.

"I should have never taken that job in Miami." Her smile is wry now, and I rub my thumb over a tear.

She seems to be waiting for my response, something to tell her that I understand, but of course, I don't.

"We can't live by our regrets," I say, a piece of truth I recently embraced on my way through time.

She swallows, and I wish I had more for her. I know it sounds like a platitude to her, but my mind is stuck on, *what happened in Miami?*

"Will you still love me if we never have another child?"

The question is so raw, and so unexpected I draw in a hard breath.

"Of course," I say. Eve had three miscarriages before we had Ashley. It's a question I answered long ago.

But she might see grief in my eyes as she lifts herself to kiss me. Still, Ashley was a surprise.

Eve just doesn't know she's still in our tomorrows.

In the sleek, velvet hours of the night, I find her, and she finds me.

Of course.

Because happiness is a person.

I'm surrendering to slumber, my body sinking like a rock into a sweet, unfamiliar oblivion, Eve's head tucked onto my shoulder when my phone ringing jars me awake.

Eve pushes herself up, and away from me and I snatch my phone off the nightstand.

The face of my partner, Andrew Burke, flashes on the screen a moment before I swipe open the call.

I don't know why, but I'm instantly awake, sitting up, my heart thumping.

His breathing makes me picture him running. "Rem, she's in labor."

It's moments like these when I have to untangle the pronouns. Track through timelines to figure out the correct response.

She. Burke's wife Shelby, current Minneapolis Police Chief ready to give birth to their first child.

"Wow, okay, um…good luck." I'm not sure what to say, really.

Especially since, in my last timeline, Shelby was dating *me*.

I reach out and touch Eve's shoulder, anchoring myself, just because.

"No—I'm in Mankato. I had a gig." A door slams behind his words.

A gig. Burke—Sticks—is a jazz drummer. Mankato? What was he thinking going to a gig that far out?

"You have to get her. Her water broke!"

"Call 911—" The sheets fall to my waist, gooseflesh forming on my skin.

Next to me, Eve's head pops up.

"I did. They put me on hold!"

I hold back a word, then push the blankets off me and turn on the light. "Got it. We're on our way."

Eve has gotten up, too, and reaches for a T-shirt.

"Take her to Southdale."

"Yeah, yeah. Just don't drive off the road." I look at the clock. It's after midnight. "I'll call you when we get there."

I hang up and toss the phone on the bed. Eve is buttoning her jeans. "What?"

"Shelby is in labor."

Her eyes widen. "But she's not due for two weeks."

"I know." I say it, but really, this is news to me. I reach for my jeans, too. "She'll be okay. We'll get there."

Her face is a little whitened, however, and I'm not sure why. "Eve—?"

And just like that, the room shifts, and for a moment, I fear I've triggered time, and it's reaching for me.

But I don't have the watch. I've lost it, somewhere between 1997 and today, and for now, I'm anchored in the now. I know you're a little bit lost, but stay with me, it's worth it. Right now, there's a more urgent matter on the stove, we've got a baby to deliver.

Except, even as the room resets, in my mind, I'm seeing Eve sitting on our bathroom floor, her face pale, the floor bloody. *I'm losing the baby.*

It's a real memory, but I don't know if it's from this time, or before.

No wonder she's pale as she grabs her shoes.

I catch up to her at the door. "Shelby is going to be fine. I promise."

Eve turns and wraps her arms around my waist, her body trembling. Then she pushes me away, and she's the Eve who is the Director of the Minneapolis Crime Lab, the woman who has won the August Vollmer Forensic Science Award (at least she did in my original life).

She knows how to handle tragedy.

Please, let this not be a tragedy.

When I open the garage door, I'm momentarily jarred by the empty stall next to Eve's car.

My vintage Porsche, my touchstone to my real life, isn't there. But I don't have time to ask as we hop in Eve's Escape. She drives to Shelby's house, a suggestion I make as I hand her the keys.

Because I haven't a clue where Burke might live.

To my surprise, less than ten minutes later she pulls up to a one-and-a-half story bungalow in the Lenox neighborhood of Minneapolis. It's a tidy place, with a stone walk and the front light is on when we arrive.

The door is open. "Shelby?" I give two quick raps on the wood, then push it open. The cop in me never likes arriving to a house with an open door, but she's probably expecting us. I push Eve behind me anyway as we step inside.

Shelby is kneeling on the floor, her arms braced on a gray sofa in the living room.

"Shelby!" Eve pushes past me.

Shelby's blonde hair is pulled back into a messy ponytail and sweat sheens her face. Her head is down, and she's breathing hard. "My water broke, and the contractions are fast and hard." She is calm, but her voice trembles. Because she might be the Minneapolis Police Chief, and a pro when it comes to handling stressful situations, but this is her first baby.

I pull up my phone and dial 911. Because from the looks of it, we don't have much time.

And I spy blood pooling on the carpet below her.

So does Eve, but she pulls a blanket around Shelby's shoulders and helps her off the floor. "Let's go."

911 is still ringing, so I hang up and pocket my phone. "Methodist Hospital is six minutes away."

And I ignore any weird protocol between my boss and me, as I pick Shelby up.

Eve follows me out and I put Shelby in the back seat. Eve slides in next to her. "You drive."

We'd left the car running, and in a moment, I'm pulling out onto Wooddale, taking the back roads.

At this time of night, the road is mine.

Four minutes, tops.

Shelby is getting loud.

Once, in my early days, I helped deliver a baby on the side of the road. It was during a pile-up, a spring storm that hit our area and John Booker and I happened to be caught in the mess of ice and snow.

And the only officers on the scene.

One of the most terrifying moments of my life, and it would have gone south if Booker hadn't been there.

"Rem, I think—"

"We're almost there!" I'm crossing Highway 7 and heading toward Alabama Avenue.

"Rem, pull over! She is having this baby, now."

"Tell her to breathe and hold it in!"

Yeah, I hear you, I can't believe I said that either.

We should have waited for help.

"Pull *over*!"

I stomp on the gas. "Hang on."

Shelby Burke and her baby are not dying on my watch.

Eve shouts and Shelby screams as I skid onto my turn onto Excelsior Boulevard.

A siren sounds behind me, and Eve is shouting and—

Rem, hurry!

The voice clangs through me, and even as Eve is shouting in

the background, her voice is fading into another voice.

No, another version of her voice. This voice is attached to her grip on my arm, and I look over to the passenger seat and Eve is there, her hand on her belly.

A belly that looks six months pregnant. She's wearing a maternity shirt, her hair is short and curly and she's younger, maybe. Her face is white. *"I can't lose another one..."*

"Look out!"

I see the road again, and it's still dark and the siren is whining, but the image is so vivid in my brain I look back again at the seat.

She's still sitting there, her eyes on me and I know, deep in my bones, this is a memory.

Just one I'm not familiar with.

I pull onto Louisiana and hit the brakes, nearly sliding under the ER canopy.

The cruiser pulls up behind me, but I ignore it and get out.

Blood covers the back of my seat, and Eve is glaring at me, but I reach in and pull Shelby out, swing her again into my arms.

The ER door slides open and I'm nearly running as Shelby writhes in my arms. "Help! We need help!"

A nurse arrives, then an intern in scrubs and I put Shelby down on the first gurney I find.

Eve takes her hand and I step back as the nurse pulls a curtain.

Then I'm standing in the hallway of the ER, adrenaline still pumping through my veins.

"Rembrandt!" My name echoes down the hallway.

I turn and see a cop heading my way. And I'm nonplussed because I know him.

Beefy Jimmy Williams, beat cop. His death, three years ago, was why I quit the force.

His death and the fact I didn't want to leave my daughter

without her father.

Sure, call it fear, but like I said, it's getting easier for me to untangle the truths from my heart.

"Is it Eve?" He glances into the room.

"Shelby."

He raises an eyebrow. "Is she going to be okay?"

We can both hear her behind the curtain, making noises that no man wants to hear.

Jimmy is quiet beside me. Then, "Sorry if this is bringing back memories for you."

I glance at him and he clamps a hand on my shoulder like we're old friends.

The curtain slides back and Shelby is hooked up to an I.V. and being wheeled out of the room. She has her eyes closed and is wearing an expression that seeps inside me to my bones.

Turns them fragile.

Eve comes out and slips her hand into mine. Watches as Shelby disappears through the door at the end of the hall. "I know you're thinking about her."

I'm silent because I know she's not talking about Shelby.

I look at her out of the corner of my eye.

She turns to me. "You can admit it, Rem." She touches my face, her eyes wet. "You can admit that you miss her."

And my body goes hard and ice cold because for a second, another memory flashes.

I'm in the hospital with Eve, sitting with her on the bed and she's holding a baby. Our baby.

Ashley.

I know this memory. Or do I?

She leans her head against my chest. "I'm trying not to think about her ... so hard. But being here, I can't keep the images away."

I swallow, and I can't take it. "Who?"

Her intake of breath tells me I've hurt her, and the look on her face is a potent mixture of pain and confusion.

And I know the answer even before Eve responds. It's no longer a feeling. It's a certainty seeping through me like a poison.

"Who do you think?" Her voice is soft, but her eyes are sharp. "Who else would I be thinking about but our daughter—"

No, please—

"Ashley."

I stare at her.

And then I see it. The tiny grave marker that has never been a part of my body of true memories.

She was here. And now she's gone. I am too late.

CHAPTER 2

Back in my early days, I met the dawn with a morning run, a workout at Quincy's gym, and a bran (okay, yeah, sometimes blueberry) muffin from the Dayton Deli.

Those days feel painfully close as I stand at the window, watching the dawn press against the windows of the skyline, glinting gold and rose.

I've been back forty-eight hours, and I'm already itching to return to the past. To find a timeline I can live in, one where my daughter still exists.

And, of course, to hunt down Leo Fitzgerald.

But I can't, remember? I nearly reach for my wrist to rub the watch, a habit I've picked up, and I recall John Booker doing the same.

Maybe he had the same itch.

"I guess this makes you chief."

I turn at Burke's statement, my hands in my pocket. I feel run over, stiff and grimy, whiskered, crabby and Eve's words from last night are still irking me. *"You've wanted this your entire life. Even before Booker died."*

Maybe. But I know, right now, taking the job of police chief is the last thing I want to do.

Not when the Jackson killer is still at large.

And not when I can't go back to stop him.

"I suppose," I say to him.

Burke is sitting behind me, in a chair, holding his newborn daughter. Fatherhood looks good on him. His little girl is a tiny football in his huge hands. She has the creamy dark skin that's an interesting mix of Burke's midnight dark and Shelby's creamy white complexions, and curious golden-brown hair that lays in tiny curlicues on her scalp. She's asleep, her lips askew, and laying on Burke's chest, skin to skin.

A whopping six pounds, three ounces, a decent size for a child born early. And she's perfect.

I nearly wept seeing her tiny fingers and toes, remembering.

Remembering is dangerous.

Shelby is asleep in the bed, hooked to an I.V., and a heart machine, her body ravaged from the preeclampsia that nearly took her life. Her blonde hair is matted, deep shadows well under her eyes, like a warrior who's taken a hard fall.

There's a ready memory tucked away that I refuse to acknowledge because Eve looked exactly this way after our Ashley, the one I know, was born. Eve had complications too, which resulted in a hysterectomy.

But we had Ashley and we were happy.

Wow, were we happy. I wish I'd realized it sooner.

Now, Eve is curled up in a nearby chair, her hands against her cheek.

With Shelby's emergency delivery, and subsequent bleeding, we couldn't just leave.

I sat in the waiting room with Burke, remembering too well

the time he did the same for me, in my real life, the one that's starting to dim, too many other memories poking holes through it.

I'm starting to harbor the fear that the fabric of my past might become too porous and the memories from this timeline will pour through.

I'll lose my Ashley for good.

Shelby is stirring, and maybe she's been awake all along because she opens her eyes and looks at me. She's on pain killers, so I don't take it personally when she says, "Don't tell me you're having second thoughts."

She has a tone I don't recognize, something of authority, and I suppose it's one she's cultivated. It calls me up, however, and I shake my head.

"Good. Because this is the wrong time to quit on me, Stone. I need a man who knows this city, and can keep a clamp on the situation with the Malakovs until I get back."

The Malakovs. I nod, and the name nudges something deep inside, but it's not a ready memory.

"They're still trying to connect the residue from the bomb to anything in Malakov's history, but we'll get it." This from Eve, who has also woken and she's gathering herself. "Alexander Malakov can't declare war on the police department and get away with it."

She looks over at me. "You'll get another Porsche, babe."

My *Porsche?*

And suddenly the image of my sweet ride in flames explodes in my memory.

That was real?

Or, well, you know what I mean.

I hadn't given it much thought, really, mostly because, well, you know, it happened two lifetimes ago.

The Malakovs. They sound Russian.

A Russian blew up my Porsche. And declared *war* on my department?

Maybe I *do* want this job.

"What about Leo Fitzgerald? Where are we on the Jackson killings?" I ask, but I keep my voice easy.

Not overly obsessed.

Burke looks up, and the baby starts to stir. Eve is watching her, wearing an expression I can't name.

"We searched Hollie Larue's body for DNA, but it came back negative."

Poor Hollie Larue. She's died twice now.

"What about Meggie Fox? You said she had DNA and a footprint."

"Meggie Fox?" Eve says. "She's not in my file."

I blink.

I hope my surprise doesn't reach my face. "Sorry. My mistake. Different case."

"Professor Gunter over at University says he thinks Jackson is getting more brazen. That his cooling off periods are becoming shorter." Eve gestures to the baby, and Burke hands her off. "He thinks he's preparing for something bigger."

My wife nearly glows with a newborn in her arms. Maybe it's because she spends so much time with death.

"Professor Gunter?" I ask. "I don't—"

"Oh, c'mon Rem. He's only been consulting on the case for the last five years. Behavioral Analyst?" She's frowning at me even as she rocks side to side.

"I'm just tired," I say.

She's still frowning, but now cooing to the baby.

Who else would I be thinking about but our daughter—? Her words are echoing in my ears now.

"Jackson isn't your job," Shelby says from her bed. "Your job is to keep my officers safe and keep Mayor Vega from getting in the way of us doing our jobs."

Mayor…Mariana Vega?

Oh, this will be fun. My last memory of her, well besides the one where she turned down my permit to build a home office over my garage, was my arrest of her son.

We're going to get along just swimmingly.

The room goes quiet, however, and Eve raises eyebrow.

"What?"

"Just try not to get yourself into a lather every time you talk to her, okay?" Shelby says and now I'm frowning at her. Me? Lather?

"Why?"

"Oh please. You haven't exactly kept your feelings to yourself about her son being paroled," Eve says.

Paroled. "Ramses Vega got *paroled?*"

"Rem—" Eve starts, and my tone might deserve it. But, cut me a break. It felt like I put the bomber in jail just a week ago. "It's been twenty-four years."

"He took twenty lives!"

Eve is still frowning. "Twelve. I mean, not that it makes a difference, since he pleaded not guilty. But…are you okay?"

Right. Twelve. Sure. Except. "Not guilty? Are you kidding?"

Eve cocks her head. "Rem, he was never convicted of the murders. The proof was inconclusive. They put him in jail for the attempted murder of a cop—you."

"What?" And shoot, of course I know this, but, really? I brace my hands on the foot of Shelby's bed. Shake my head. "Yes. Right."

"This is what I'm talking about. You can't come unglued every time Vega's name is mentioned," Shelby says.

I hold up my hands. If time travel has taught me anything, it's that I need to keep my mouth shut and a lid on my gut reactions. "I'll behave." I hold up two fingers. "Scout's honor."

Burke is grinning at that, giving a little shake of his head. "That'd be better if you'd ever been a scout."

"So, who's heading up the Jackson cases?" I ask. Because last go-round, I was in charge.

"Hey! I'm just taking a day of parental leave. Sheesh. I've still got this," Burke says.

Burke's in charge. This I can live with.

Shelby nods. "And Zeke will keep Burke in the know if anything changes."

"Zeke?"

Again, the name sounds familiar. And I get it before they have to remind me. Zeke Kincaid. A kid I mentored after I put his father in prison.

"You gotta cut the kid some slack, Rem. He's good. Smart. And he looks at you like you used to look at Booker," Burke says.

I remember seeing myself in him. Eager. Maybe a bit of a troublemaker. I liked him.

"He wants so much to be like you, he even bought a 1997 Porsche 911," Eve says. "You have to admit, sometimes he even dresses like you. I think you have a groupie in Zeke Kincaid."

The baby is starting to fuss, hungry.

Burke stands, and helps adjust Shelby's pillows. "Rem, maybe it's time to let go of this a little."

"Let go of—"

"You've looked so hard at Leo Fitzgerald, you've lost focus. You've let it consume you. These killings aren't personal. It's not a game he's playing with you."

I don't know why, but the words from Burke sting.

Except, he's probably right.

Just because my actions birthed a killer doesn't mean I'm in the ring with him.

He's a killer. I'm the Inspector trying to find him. That's all.

And now, maybe I'm passing that off to Burke.

Maybe.

"This guy Fitzgerald might not even be good for the killings," Shelby says. "Even Eve is starting to wonder if you have the right guy."

"Really?" I look at her and she doesn't meet my eyes.

Silence, and she finally looks up at me. "He's just…he's a ghost. And there are things that don't add up."

"Like what—"

She raises her hand. "Rem, we've talked about this."

No, actually, we haven't. But I can read her face. She doesn't want a showdown here.

Maybe she's right.

In fact, as I look at Burke and his baby, his sweet family, I wonder what my investigation—notice I didn't say obsession, but I can get focused, we all know that—has cost me in this lifetime.

I glance at Eve. No, what it has cost us.

So, I sigh, and nod. "I'll let Burke run the show."

Because, really, they're right. This isn't personal.

"You'll be great, Rem. Just, keep the place running until I get back. Six weeks, tops," Shelby says, her gaze landing on her daughter, then Burke. Now, she gives him a smile that tells me we're interlopers.

"C'mon, Eve," I say as she hands off the baby.

Eve settles her into her mother's arms. Lets her touch linger on the baby's head.

I take her hand, and she grips it as we start to walk out.

"Hey, Rem. Don't forget the press conference today," Shelby

says when I reach the door.

I nod. Sure. Probably about Jackson. I've been here before.

When we walk out, Eve is silent for a long time. We find the elevator and I hit the button.

"I can't do it, Rem."

I look at her and she's wearing an odd look, her eyes watery.

Oh no—

"I can't keep trying. I think…I think we should just stop."

I freeze, because deep in my bones, I know what she's saying.

"I can't go through losing another child. And I don't want to risk it."

I draw in a breath, and her question is hanging there. *"Will you still love me if we never have another child?"*

Of course.

The words hollow me out, however, as I pull her close.

Never have another child? Never hear the laughter of a little girl, see the look in her eyes when I come home, have her throw herself into my arms? Never hold her when she cries, stand at her bedside when she's hurt…never find myself tiptoeing into her room at night to watch her dream?

Of course.

The elevator dings, but I don't care who sees us. My world is imploding, and I need someone to hold onto.

Yet, someone has stepped out and I feel the presence behind me even before a voice says, "Boss? You okay?"

I let Eve go and turn.

Zeke.

I *remember* him.

The relief at this carry over from my last timeline is so rich I nearly gasp. He's in his mid-twenties and wears his hair in a man bun. He's built—I remember going a round with him down at

Quincy's. He has moves and can handle himself and like I said, he reminds me of me.

I used to think that was a good thing.

He's wearing jeans and a black T-shirt, his badge hanging around his neck, but he's unshaven and looks like he dressed fast. "Sorry to interrupt. Everything okay with the chief?"

I nod. We've come through a secure area, so I'm not sure what he's doing here. Except, Shelby's words are hanging in my head. "*Zeke will keep Burke in the know if anything changes.*"

"Do you need to see Burke?"

He is looking past me, then back. Nods.

"What's going on?"

He hesitates, then, "We found more of them. Lots more."

His words are shuffling around in my head. More of…

"Except these are old. Really old. Like, twenty years or more old."

"Zeke," Eve says, putting a hand on his arm. "What are you talking about?"

I could kiss her.

"The Jackson murders. We got an anonymous tip last night that there were more bodies and we drove out there this morning." His mouth tightens. "We found the first one about an hour ago. And Silas and the CSI team found four more on my way here."

"Four more bodies."

"Five," Eve the math whiz says.

Five bodies. "Where?" I feel myself shaking, even as Eve curls her hand over my arm.

"On an abandoned farm outside of Waconia."

Even as he says it, something doesn't feel right, a coldness seeping through me.

And that's when Zeke stumbles. His mouth is trying to form

the words—it opens, then closes, then opens again and finally, "It's your farm, Rembrandt. The farm you grew up on. All of the bodies are buried in your backyard."

CHAPTER 3

This must be my fault. Something I've changed in the past. I have no other explanation.

No one realizes this but me, of course, but the weight of it sinks into me as I stand on the edge of my family farm, watching the crime scene team dig up the past. Cadaver dogs roam the field, sniffing for more remains, as well as CSIs with ground penetrating radar machines.

I'm holding my breath.

You know how it is when you're standing on the sidelines, your body buzzing as you glance at the coach, hoping he'll put you in the game? That feeling that simmers deep inside when you know, with every thump of your heart, that if you just get your hands on the ball you can smash through the defense into the end zone?

I'm seventeen, antsy, adrenaline hot inside me as I stand on the sidelines watching Silas O'Roarke and his crime scene team dig up the small field behind the house I grew up in.

Leo Fitzgerald has killed my daughter, and now, he's trying to put the blame on me.

You'd be restless and crabby, too.

It's mid-morning, and the sun casts a shadow from the dilapidated yellow house that holds my memories. The porch is sagging, an old geranium pot, discarded, laying on its side.

The barn is weathered, the doors open, and old memories blow out. I can almost hear my father's old felt-covered transistor radio playing the classic rock that embeds my bones, Bryan Adams singing, "Ain't No use in Complainin'."

I want to ask Eve what happened to my parents. But I can't. It would sound too strange.

Last time I saw them, my mother served Eve pancakes in the eat-in kitchen just off the front porch.

My dad helped me dig my Jeep out of storage after a snow-storm.

It was good. Really, really good.

Eve is out in the field, garbed up in her CSI attire—gloves, protective shoe covers and a jacket identifying her. She's head of the entire department, so the underlings in the field defer to her as she checks on their progress.

A team of twelve is exhuming five bodies, carefully, taking pictures, logging evidence, the scale of the crime scene overwhelming.

I have too many questions to begin, so I'm watching, but turning over what I know.

The murders started sometime after my first jump back in time, to the summer of 1997 when I stopped Ramses Vega from blowing up a third coffee shop in his political protest.

The Jackson killer's first victim was his own girlfriend, a cocktail waitress named Lauren Delany.

She held a worn twenty in her grip, the eerie words, *thank you for your service*, written in black ink across the face of the bill. Hence, the nickname—Jackson, as in Andrew, whose face is on the twenty.

Eve found Leo Fitzgerald's DNA on the body, finally, and tied to him to the crime in the recent past.

His second victim was a nurse named Gretchen Anderson. Same MO. Same twenty-dollar tip. And, she dated Fitzgerald.

We know it's him. We just can't seem to get ahead of him.

Most of the victims have been in their late teens or early twenties, all of them strangled, sexually assaulted. The most recent victim, a girl named Hollie Larue, survived his first attempt, but died during my last rewrite of history.

And this one, apparently.

In earlier days, Fitzgerald killed John Booker in an ambush-explosion at an abandoned house three years ago.

And, most importantly, Fitzgerald murdered my four-year-old daughter, at least once.

This time around, I'm not sure how she died, but the fact that Leo has deposited his kills in my backyard doesn't bode well.

Unfortunately, my past creates a puzzle of disjointed pieces that don't all fit together.

A rusty swing set squeaks in the scant morning breeze, the smell of summer in the greening, overgrown lawn, the weedy remains of a garden.

I'm standing with my arms folded, watching the activity, my thoughts taking me through time, when Eve walks up to me.

"Rem. You okay?"

I look at her. She's not the woman who held onto me at the hospital, her fears overtaking her. This Eve wears her auburn hair tied back and a grim, but clinical expression in her pretty hazel green eyes. She's focused, the emotions from earlier in the day buried.

"Why would he pick my parents' home to bury these women?"

She raises a shoulder. "But there's something more—these remains are old, like Zeke said. Twenty or more years."

I shake my head. "Eve, I would have noticed if someone buried bodies in our backyard."

"That's the thing. They were moved here within the last three years. After your parents moved to Florida."

My parents moved to Florida. Relief floods me.

"This house doesn't even belong to them anymore. It's owned by the city of Waconia, slated to be demolished."

I don't know why that pinches. It wasn't like I have a full deck of happy memories here. Most of my childhood was spent mourning for my brother, Mickey, kidnapped when I was twelve.

Still. Demolished. It feels like a keen metaphor for my life.

"So, someone killed these women, and then, seventeen years later dug them up and moved them? How do you know?"

She makes a face. "The bodies are in garbage bags, the bones, clothing and other epidermal remains all…well, the bodies were already decomposed when they were transferred. The graves are not large enough for entire bodies…"

I understand what she's getting at. "How are you determining how long they've been here?"

"We'll sample the earth around it, determine how much electrical resistivity is in the soil. In a…fresh body, the conductivity in the soil water significantly increases up to two years after burial. But, like I said, these bodies were in lawn bags, so we're also looking at the breakdown of the plastic, and of course the make of the bag."

I look at her. "Do they match the profile? Are you sure these are Jackson kills?"

She nods, then holds up a bag. It's been numbered and labeled but as she hands it to me, I am without breath.

A faded twenty-dollar bill marked with the tell-tale words.

I hand it back to her, and something akin to nausea rises inside.

Five more women.

One thought, however, pulses in the back of my brain even as my phone vibrates in my jeans pocket.

If these kills happened over twenty years ago, then it's possible they didn't start after the coffee shop bombing.

But in my original timeline, that's where they ended.

You know what this means, right?

This may not be my fault. Or at least, not entirely.

I'm not sure why, but I don't feel any better.

"Thanks, Eve," I say as I pull out my phone. "Stone here."

I don't recognize the voice on the other end.

"I expected you in my office ten minutes ago so we could prepare."

Not a clue. "Sorry. I was called to a scene—"

"Save it, Stone. We have a press conference in an hour and you'd better not stand me up."

Press conference. And I blame my stellar investigative skills—and my history with this woman—for my quick response. "Sorry, Mayor Vega. I'm on my way."

"Wear a suit."

She hangs up, and I think I handled that pretty well, considering our past.

But I'm still attired in my jeans and T-shirt from last night, so maybe she's right.

"The mayor," Eve says, and one eyebrow lifts. "Lucky you."

"I guess I have a press conference today." I remember my last one, in a not-too-distant lifetime. That time, I was giving an update on the Jackson killer, and Eve wasn't talking to me.

This time she gives me a kiss on the cheek as I leave. "Be the charmer I remember."

I don't think I was ever a charmer, but I'll take the kiss. I leave in her car and head back to the house, take a shower, change into a requisite suit and pull into the downtown ramp with minutes to spare.

The downtown headquarters is located in a beautiful rose granite building constructed in 1888. I park in the ramp and take the tunnel, coming out at the center rotunda. The giant sculpture of Neptune of the Sea sits in the center of the room, under the five-story rotunda, and I rub his big toe for luck as I walk by.

I find the mayor's office and her assistant knocks and lets me right in.

The last time I met Mariana Vega in the past, I'd chased her son through uptown, tackled him and we had a little tussle. She wasn't happy.

It's been twenty-four years for her, but her expression of annoyance hasn't aged a day as she rises from the chair behind her massive black desk. Awards, plaques and pictures line her wall. Most of them feature her with various business owners around town.

Mayor Vega wears a dark-patterned V-necked wrap dress, her long brown hair up, and her dark eyes hold no quarter as she holds out her hand. "Chief Stone."

That's sounds weird, right? I'm not the only one?

I meet her hand, and the handshake is ever so brief before she drops it. "Sit."

I feel like her pet mastiff, so I stay standing.

Maybe this is what Shelby means about behaving myself.

"Suit yourself," Vega says as she sits. She folds her hands on the desk. "You should know that you weren't my first choice."

Knock me over with a stick. "I'm sure."

"But Chief Burke says you're the one to fill her shoes." She says this as if her mouth is full of bile. "We just need to make something clear if we're going to work together."

I'm trying to read her. She's put on weight with age, her cheeks rounder, her chin thicker, but she's still a striking woman.

The kind that you probably don't want to get on the wrong side of, so I keep my mouth shut.

"Stop harassing my son."

Great. I'm apparently still at it. And here I had this fantasy it was going to be easier.

"Mayor Vega, I don't know what you're talking about." And, really, I'm not lying here, am I?

"Please. You've driven by our house every single night for a week. Well, until your Porsche was torched." She leans forward. "Which he didn't do."

I remember what Shelby said about some Russian gang blowing up my beloved Porsche, but with Mariana's words, it occurs to me that I might want to take a closer look at her son.

"What was he in jail for again?" I raise an eyebrow even as she purses her mouth. "Oh that's right—bombing." I lean forward, my hands on her desk. "How did you manage this, anyway? To become *mayor.*"

Eve's in my head, *Be the charmer I know you to be.* I haven't a clue who she might be referring to.

Vega is on her feet. "Inspector Stone—"

"Chief," I say and sit down. "Your son murdered twelve people," I got that right this time. "How he is out on parole has to be a question for the ethics committee."

She's wearing a face that looks similar to the time I called her and her entire city council a bunch of communists for not allowing me to build my garage addition.

Thankfully, that's not in her memory in this timeline. At least I don't think so. But she's having none of it, her voice shaking a little as she rises. "My son wasn't convicted of the bombings, Stone, and you know it. He's done his time. He's a changed man, and it's time he was free."

I stay seated, and keep my voice even, soft. "I don't know who blew up my Porsche. But if Ramses did it, then you and I both know he's dangerous. And the last place he should be is walking the streets." I take in a deep breath. "Mariana. He bombed two coffee shops. And would have kept going—."

"He was innocent." She meets my eyes, unflinching. "Someone set him up."

Wow, she really believes that.

"Who?"

"You never got the bomb-maker, did you?"

I don't know, but my guess is no, from her expression.

"But you don't care about that. You just want to put blame on the son of an immigrant."

I shake my head and rise. I rise. "I'm watching him." Although, it's probably an empty threat.

I have bigger piranha on my plate.

As if reading my mind, she folds her arms, looks back at me. "Tell me where we are with the Jackson murders."

I'm not sure what Burke had told her—or maybe me, before I took this job. But, "We found five bodies today, out in a field in Waconia. It's not in our jurisdiction, but they all have the Jackson signature twenty-dollar bills with their remains, so..."

She grits her teeth. "Perfect. Were there reporters there?"

I frown. "I didn't see any."

"Good. This gets out, it'll only start a panic."

I'm starting to panic. "Wait—doesn't the public know?"

In my last timeline, we told the public. And it saved lives. Or, at least one life. Hollie Larue.

Until, of course, it didn't.

Vega is looking at me like I've suggesting setting Vikings stadium on fire. "That's the last thing we want to do."

I lean over her desk. "No, Mayor, the last thing we want is for more women to die."

"Which means you have to catch him, Stone. And if we give out details, we'll have copycats starting up everywhere."

"We need to warn people."

We're staring at each other, and probably that's why we don't hear her assistant knock, or the door open. Just her voice, "Madam Mayor, it's time for the press conference."

She glances at the woman, nods, then looks back at me. "No press. But I do want daily updates."

I purse my lips, but nod, turn and head for the door. Her voice stops me.

"So? What are you going to say?"

I turn. "Um," And I haven't a clue what she's talking about. I want to say, 'Who's on First,' but she's looking at me like I'm a child, and the strangest hint of compassion enters her eyes.

"I know this is hard for you, Rembrandt. But you volunteered, so…" She comes around the desk and reaches for a light sweater hanging on the hook. "I know whatever you say, it will be the right thing."

The right thing?

She opens the door, and somehow, I move my feet toward the door.

"Besides, he did die saving your life."

Her hand pats my shoulder as we walk out of her office, and

my brain is scrambling.

Who died?

She descends the marble staircase toward the rotunda and walks across the marble floor through to the annex of the administrative offices of the Minneapolis Police Department.

We enter a lobby filled with wall plaques and awards and head toward a row of busts of past police chiefs. One is covered in a black cloth.

My entire body heats up. I think I know.

A crowd of reporters and other attendees—many of them officers in uniform—are gathered.

A podium is set up in front, and Mayor Vega steps up to it.

It's then I see the picture. An oil painting leaning beside the cloth-covered bust.

The likeness of the man who died *saving my life*.

Chief of Police, John Booker.

CHAPTER 4

I nail the press conference. Because like Eve said, I'm a charmer.

Who knew, really, but I stepped up to the podium, after Mayor Vega introduced me, realizing that while I haven't a clue how Booker died, I *do* know him.

Maybe better than anyone, really.

So, I got this, and maybe Queen's "Don't Stop Me Now," is playing in my head—I almost feel supersonic as people laugh at my stories and finally clap to my words. Then they unveil the bust, and the likeness of Booker seems accurate. Sort of a craggy, old west character with pensive eyes and a grim set to his mouth, with just a tweak of a smile, who deserves merit in our history.

Booker was the man I most wanted to be like.

I pose for a few pictures, glad-hand people I don't know and mingle until I finally peel off and make for the door.

I just might nail this police chief gig.

I'm nearly free when Mayor Vega's voice hisses in my wake. "What the hell was *that*?"

I turn, and she's coming at me, eyes hot.

Claws in, you cat, but I don't say that. Instead I clear the door and duck into a nearby hallway. Although with these marble floors and walls, my guess is that any reporter with a good ear could listen in on this showdown.

"What?" I say and really, what's she so irked about? There was joking. Stories. I told about the time that Booker drove one of the squad cars into the lake on a chase. And the time he delivered a baby on the side of the road. (Remember? I told you that one already.)

"Really, Stone? Not one mention of the fact he caught a serial killer?"

I'm just staring at her, because I have no memory of a serial killer—or Booker catching him, in my timeline.

She cocks her head, one dark eyebrow in a frown.

"The Grays Lake murderer. Please. Of all people, you're the one person who I thought would want to mention that accolade."

My heart is thundering in my ears.

There's only one Grays Lake I know of…the one where my brother, Michelangelo was discovered some, well, twenty-four years ago.

In that timeline, the murderer was still undiscovered.

I can't speak and she rolls her eyes. "In fact, I would have thought it would have been the main subject of your speech."

"Because of my brother?" I say quietly.

"Listen, I know you probably want to downplay it, but we both know that's what sold all those books of yours. The kid whose brother was taken becomes a cop and works with the man who solved the case?" She raises an eyebrow.

Right. "I just wanted people to know him like I did," I say, trying to keep up.

Booker, what did you do? Because remember, I got the watch

from him. And my brother's murder was one of *his* cold cases.

Except, in this timeline, apparently, he's solved it.

That cheater. Booker is rewriting *my* timeline, and I don't like it.

"Plus, half those things didn't even happen," she says. "Delivered a baby? Right."

I shrug, because what am I going to say?

"I've got my eye on you, Stone." She turns and walks away, her heels clipping on the marble.

I wrap a hand around my neck, kneading a stiff muscle. I need coffee.

I find a kiosk outside and order a latte before heading back to my office, down in the police department wing. The reporters have left, and I stand for a moment in front of Booker's bust. I can almost hear his voice. *"Did you give me a good eulogy?"*

Yes, I did, boss. Yes, I did.

I find my way back to the administrative offices. Booker's was always number 103, and that's where I go, bypassing a secretary, a man sitting outside the door. "This mine?" I ask before I go in. I read his name—Reagan.

He's young and tidy, crew cut, sharp shouldered. Probably on the ball. He stands. "Yes, sir. I finished cleaning it out this morning. It's ready for you."

I open my door.

"Sir—there's a—"

"I see her," I say as I spot a woman sitting on the sofa in the room. She's young, maybe mid-twenties, with shoulder-length wavy brown hair and deep brown eyes. She's wearing a gray jacket, a pair of dress pants and heels. And most importantly, a press pass around her neck.

She looks familiar, but I know I've never met her before. I

41

don't close the door. "Hello?"

She rises. "That was amazing, Rembrandt. I didn't know half those things about John." It almost looks like she's been crying, her eyes reddened. "Thanks for that."

Clearly, we know each other, and thankfully, her name is on her pass. I'm not trying to be creepy, but my gaze flickers down to her badge.

Frankie Dale. Star-Trib *reporter*.

"Can I help you?" I ask.

Behind her, the windows open up to a view of the skyline, and in case I'm not sure when I am, the sun is glinting off the silvery sloped dome of the Minnesota Vikings stadium so it's probably noon; and I'm starved.

Mostly, I want to find Eve.

And hide.

No, not really, but maybe a little.

"John would have been really proud," Frankie says.

"Thank you." I wait for her to continue but she doesn't. So, "Do we have an appointment?"

She frowns, but then nods. "You said I could shadow you on your first day. Just to do an informal report on our new chief of police."

Uh, no. Not a chance. Sorry, but who out there thinks this is a good idea?

"I don't think so."

"I won't get in the way."

I hold up a hand. "Not today."

"But—"

"No!" And I don't mean it quite as emphatically as it comes out, so I cut my voice down. "Listen. It's not a good day, okay?"

"Why not?"

Really? I don't know why, but her tone has set off a fuse inside me. Call it fatigue—after all, I barely slept. And then there was the field of dead bodies. And maybe just a little the niggling fact that Ashley is dead again, and I don't know how.

So yeah, I'm struggling to be charming. "I have too much going on." I shake my head and walk over to my desk.

She follows me. "Rembrandt. Talk to me."

Her voice is soft, and I have the weirdest feeling that I know her well. Too well?

Not good.

"I'll keep it off the record. You know that. But...is it the Jackson killer?" Her expression is almost kind, and it unnerves me.

She gives me a wounded half smile. "You know I know."

I do? And I'm not sure why—maybe the way she doesn't move. Maybe the way she swallows, looking like I've hurt her. Maybe it's just that this woman seems to know me—well enough to call me by my name—and I haven't a clue who she is, but weirdly, I feel like I trust her.

Even so, yelling erupts in the back of my head—*shut up, Rem!*—as the words escape. "Listen, I have a gang that has declared war on policemen, a guy on parole who should still be locked up, a mayor who is out to get me, a field of dead bodies and—"

Whoops.

Her eyes have gone wide.

"It's the Jackson killer, right?"

Great. Day one on the job and I've already blown it. "I can't talk about it. And...you have to go. I can't—"

"But you found more bodies."

"We're done." I come around the desk. The door is still open. "Go."

She's giving me a hard stare, then shakes her head. "You know

I'll find out anyway."

I'm not sure if that's a threat, a statement, or a promise. But I stand at the door, holding it, waiting.

"Fine."

The look she gives me as she leaves again feels so laced with a familiar disgust that I'm just a little shaken as I close the door.

This is why I shouldn't be chief. Did no one remember I wrote a memoir about my first year as an investigator? I am not good at secrets.

Let's be honest. It's a small miracle that I've kept my mouth shut about my time travel so far.

I can't face whatever pile of work is on my desk, so after a few minutes, I leave and head over to the Dayton Deli, grab a couple ham salad sandwiches and return to Eve's office.

I know I've been here thousands of times, but this feels new as I walk in. She's got her own office that overlooks 3rd Street, but the room is filled with stainless steel tables, white boards, workstations and computers. A group of younger CSI techs are garbed in gloves and masks, labeling and examining evidence.

I'm so proud of Eve. She's worked hard to become the woman she is today. Although in this timeline, some of that work was in Miami.

We're not done with that conversation, I promise you.

Silas is in an adjacent office. He's the deputy CSI director, and one of Eve's best friends. He looks up as I pass his office. Neither of us smile.

He's never liked me, so of course he backed up me when she wanted to divorce me two timelines ago. I've always believed that Silas would have stepped into the void if Eve and I called it quits, and I believe he still has it in him.

Eve is at her desk. I knock on the open door and she looks up as I hold up the bag.

"It could be called creepy the way you can read my mind."

This time, I'm innocent. But I smile and wink at her and realize that suddenly I don't feel quite so peeved with my day. This life.

I've been rolling what-ifs through my head all day, thinking about the watch. But this is the best version of my life I've returned to, and you saw what happened last time I tried to fix something.

I can probably live with this version. Like I said, it's *almost* right.

"Rembrandt Stone."

The voice comes from a man standing near her bookshelf. Tall and wiry, Norwegian in his complexion and thinning hair, blue eyes. He looks like he's spent his life indoors and he's holding a book.

I know him, although the recognition takes a moment. "Professor Gunter?"

"I hear you've been promoted to police chief," he says and switches hands so he can shake mine.

"It's just a short-term gig."

"You're just in time, Rem," Eve says. "I was going to call you. Professor Gunter came in with a theory about our serial killer."

It wouldn't be the first time I pulled in help from the behavioral analyst, so maybe he's a regular.

He puts the book down on Eve's desk as she unwraps her sandwich. I offer him mine, but he waves me off.

"I brought you my book on the psychology of serial killers," he says. "But Eve already has it on her shelf."

"A little light reading," she says as she takes a bite.

I pull up a chair and open my sandwich.

Gunter smirks and puts his hand on his book. "I think what you have here is a power-based killer. I was looking at your victims.

All of them are in service professions—bartenders, waitresses, a couple Uber drivers, and a number of, ahem, ladies of the night."

I look at Eve and she's hiding a smile.

"I believe Jackson wants to exert his power over these women. He waits for them, runs them down and overpowers them. Strangulation is a very personal crime. It takes time—and the killer must watch as the life drains from the victim's face. Most of the kills happen with the killer astride the victim, his thumbs on her throat, like this."

He makes to reach for me to demonstrate but I hold up a hand. "I get it."

"Yes, well, okay." He smooths his tie. "Because of this, these types of killers enjoy watching the police hunt them. They like to make the investigators feel powerless by sending them notes, and even leaving fake clues." He looks at Eve, and back to me. "They like to play games."

I'm not hungry anymore. "Like burying murdered women in the yard where I spent my childhood."

He nods.

I grab my coffee and lean back in my chair. "Why me? I'm not the only one working this case."

Eve caps her water bottle after taking a drink. "Rembrandt, you've been hunting this guy for…well, I remember the first time you told me about him. Over twenty years ago."

"Me too." I meet her eyes and smile.

She doesn't. "And the next day, you drove out to a bar in Montrose and beat the guy up."

Gunter looks at me. "You assaulted him?"

I hold up my hands. "Believe me, the guy can handle himself. He's ex-military."

I unconsciously reach up to touch the tiny scar on my forehead.

Gunter looks at my uneaten half of sandwich. "You gonna eat that?"

"Knock yourself out." I push it toward him.

He takes a bite. "Ham salad. My favorite."

"Eve says you think he's getting ready to do something big. A stunt. Why?"

He swallows. Nods. "Because although his kills are coming faster, you still haven't mentioned him in the media. He wants to be noticed by you. To have you call him out and pay attention to his handiwork. He wants you to play his game."

"Could these women be the big stunt?"

"How did you know they were there?"

"Zeke said it was an anonymous tip to the 911 line," Eve says.

"Can they track the call?" Gunter asks.

Eve nods. "We can try."

He takes another bite of the sandwich. I stare out the window. The sky has turned dark, gray clouds jockeying for position. The air feels thick and heavy.

"He's made this personal." Gunter finishes off the sandwich and wipes his mouth. "So be careful, because he's intelligent."

Yeah, well, so am I. And I have three versions of the past I can access to find him.

And you'd better believe, if you thought I cheated before, you haven't seen anything yet.

If I'm going to stick around in this world, then I'm going to make sure it's safe to live in.

CHAPTER 5

I'm at the gym, beating up a heavy bag.

Quincy's has always been my refuge. It's an old warehouse with high ceilings, open piping, and the sounds of guys, mostly, hitting things—each other, as well as heavy and speed bags—all punctuated with the hard thud of free weights dropping onto the black rubber mats place throughout the gym.

Inside struggles being worked out on the outside.

I'm sweating, I smell bad, my muscles hurt and I just have to keep punching until I sort this out.

The problem is, and maybe you've noticed, is that I've started to think of myself as a time traveler. Started to believe that everything I see here is not fixed but rather simply a chess piece I can move if I think through it hard enough. I'll just go back in time and dodge some things, show up for others and maybe I return to a world where everything is put right.

I don't need to get back to my timeline. I know that's long gone. I just need a world I can live in. I'll take any world where my daughter is still alive.

But what if I go back, in some—yet again—desperate attempt

to change things, and I return to an unthinkable darkness.

This alternative sends a cold finger down my spine despite the heat I'm pumping through my body.

It doesn't matter, though, does it? I can't do anything without the watch. Booker is dead, he didn't give me the watch, and that's the end of it, isn't it?

Which puts me in the conundrum of trying to figure out how to live in this world. And before you say, *What's your problem, Rem? Why do you always have to change things?* I'd like to remind you that I'm a guy. We fix things. And a detective. We solve things. And deep down inside, I'm also still a writer. (I don't know if that urge ever leaves.) And writers like to analyze things, pick them apart, find the deeper layers.

So I'm stuck in this grayscale, no man's world of not being sure of what I want to do. And frustrated that I don't have a choice.

The bag shudders as I pound it.

"That kind of day, huh?"

I catch the bag and turn, breathing hard.

Eve is standing behind me, her satchel over her shoulder, her hair a little damp from the drizzle outside.

She's so pretty I lose my breath, and it's all I can do not to walk over and kiss her. But I smell pretty bad, so—

"I just need to figure some things out."

She was smiling, but now it falls, and she nods, looks down. "Are we going to talk about it?"

About—? Fitzgerald? The fact that it's gotten personal? Or maybe Mayor Vega's hatred of me? Maybe the weird conversation with Frankie the reporter? Or, how about the fact I had to take an Uber to the gym because my *Porsche got blown up*?

Yeah, that irks me more than I thought it would. As a time traveler—there, I said it again—we need touch points to our real world.

My Porsche has been with me since the beginning.

This is the most unjointed I've felt after a return from the past. Like I'm standing in quicksand. Maybe it's because I know, this time, I'm staying.

I think.

The one sure thing I have, however, is Eve. I can live without my Porsche, right?

I've taken too long to answer and now Eve looks up at me. "Right. Okay." She sighs. "I know you blame me, Rem."

"Uh…" I frown, give a shake of my head. "Eve—"

"It's okay. Let's just go."

She looks away, and wipes a tear from her cheek.

How did we get here?

"Eve—C'mon. What's going on?"

She looks at me then, something fractured in her eyes. "Really?"

Um.

"I know you haven't forgiven me for Miami, okay? And I get it." She takes a breath. "I haven't forgiven myself, either."

What the hell happened in Miami? But I take a step toward her, despite my emanating odor, and catch her hand with my glove. "Babe. Of course I forgive you." Because whatever it is, the answer is yes. "It's done."

She meets my eyes, and my strong Eve is breaking, a fracture deep inside. What—? "Like I said, let's just *go*. Please," she says and steps away from me.

Sorry, but I've been through too many lifetimes to just let this sit.

Besides, remember what I said about fixing things?

"Eve, let's talk about it."

"No. It's in the past, and we promised never to talk about it, ok?" She holds up her hands. "I shouldn't have brought it up."

Aw. "Listen, Eve—"

"Do you want me to wait for you, or do you want to take an Uber home?"

Right.

"Let me change. I'll be right out."

She's leaning against the wall, near the door, absently running the heart charm on her necklace along the chain when I emerge, freshly showered, but unshaven, my hair wet. It's a familiar gesture, and usually precedes one of her eureka moments.

Outside, the rain is starting to pelt the parking lot and when she sees me, Eve pockets her phone and runs out to her Escape before I can circle back around to our conversation.

The radio is on in the car and I get the hint.

Maybe Burke knows what went down in Miami.

"I ordered wings from Gino's," she says and pulls into a pizza joint just a few blocks from our house. I run in and grab the order.

We drive in silence to the house.

I wonder why I haven't remodeled it yet. In my original time, I had embarked on a whole-house overhaul that included new flooring, a bigger, updated kitchen and restoring the original woodwork to its natural oak shine.

The rain is coming down in sheets as we pull in.

I can't help but look at the empty stall as I get out. In fact, I stand there, looking at the space.

Eve stops on the stoop to the inner door. "Sorry about your Porsche," she says, and I look over.

The woman can read my mind. And the fact that she's married to me in this lifetime suddenly strikes me as a gift.

Whatever happened in Miami made her return to me. Maybe

I don't want to know.

Maybe I should just accept the life I've been given.

"It's just a car."

"No, it's not. You restored it with your father. It's a lot more than just a car."

Now there's heat in my chest. "Shelby seems to think it was an attack by a Russian gang."

"Pipe bomb under your tire in the parking lot of the station. Could have been worse—no one was injured."

"Do you think Ramses Vega could have done it?" I head toward the house and she goes inside, taking off her shoes at the door.

"I don't know. He's always been angry at you, but—that was twenty some years ago."

"Mariana says he's mentally unstable. And a victim. That we never caught the real bomber."

She takes the wings from me. "No, we never caught the bomb-maker. He's the bomber, or at least the one who set them. You got him cold, Rem."

"If only we could have made it stick."

She touches my cheek. Smiles. "I know."

I think we're going to be okay.

"What do you mean, the bomb-maker?" I take off my shoes and follow her into the kitchen.

She looks over her shoulder, and frowns. "You thought that Vega wasn't smart enough to build the bombs. He didn't have the training. It had to be someone else, right?"

True. I nod, because I think I did say this.

"In fact, I don't think you ever completely closed the case. It might be in your cold case files in your office."

My cold case files in my office.

She's pulling down plates, as I head into my den. I didn't see the file box before, but now I find it under my desk, shoved way in the back. I pull out the cases.

Is it weird that I feel like I've found old friends, like looking through a yearbook, pulling out memories?

I pull out the box and sit on my leather chair, taking out the stack of manila files.

The coffee shop bombings are not there. Neither is Danny's and Asher's murder. But I do find Lauren Delaney, however, and Gretchen Anderson, Fitzgerald's girlfriend.

I pause on her file, at her picture. A nurse practitioner. Ironically, she assisted the intern who sewed up my stitches after Leo and I threw down at the bar in Montrose.

How did she get mixed up with him?

And, weirdly, she doesn't fit the profile, does she?

And then I see the date of her death. December 1997. No, that's not right. She should have died in January of 2000.

Something happened that moved her death up by two years. I put her file aside and keep flipping through the other files. Honestly, I'm searching for Ashley's file—it wasn't here last time, but I've learned not to take anything for granted—and my gaze lands on a file with Booker's name on it. I pull it out.

Eve has come into the room holding a beer. "Your wings are getting cold."

I open the folder. "Booker saved my life." I mean it more as a question, but of course I should know this.

The police report is on the front page, and I read a quick summary even as Eve says, "I nearly lost you that day. If Booker hadn't seen the guy coming out of the back room—"

The summary says that it was late, and we were at a diner when we heard an alarm sound from a nearby liquor store. That I ran outside while Booker called it in. And that while I went to investigate and help the victim, the robber emerged from the back of the store, gun in hand.

Booker arrived just in time to tackle me. The bullet grazed me on its way to his heart.

I've lost my appetite, my hand over my mouth as I'm reading. And, when I look up, I'm wrecked. "He died in my place."

Listen, I know he's been dead for years, but I just saw him two days ago and…it's not supposed to end like this, right? My chest tightens, my throat thick.

Sheesh.

She crouches in front of me. Touches my face. It's cold from her beer. "You were like a son to him. And I know how much you admired him."

She puts her other hand on my cheek. "He used to tell me that you reminded him of himself, when he was young. And how he wished he could have found your brother in time."

I'm studying her face, but really, I'm thinking of Booker, and a lecture he gave me, once upon a lifetime. *Here are the rules. The biggest one, the one that is never, ever to be broken…don't change the past.*

I can't help but shake my head. *You old dog, you. You totally went back and changed the past.*

Caught Mickey's killer.

"He used to say you had killer instincts. That you were born to be a detective. That it was a gift from God."

I raise an eyebrow.

"He got a little religious after you were stabbed by Vega. I think it scared him." She winks. "He was such a softie around you."

Softie? John *Booker?*

"But I agree with him," Eve continues. "Dad used to say the same thing. That justice was a sacred calling."

Huh.

"Booker called me a coward, once. Did you know that?" I ask quietly. And of course, this happened in a timeline she hasn't lived in, but still.

She frowns, shook her head.

"Yeah. I was going to…well, quit the force." I don't why I need to tell her this, but the story sits in my chest fighting to be coughed out. "I'd seen an officer killed, someone just shy of his retirement, and it…it got in my head, you know? And I'd seen someone I cared about grow up without their father, and I thought…I don't want that to be me."

She is looking at me a little funny. "Was this before or after Miami?"

Miami again, huh?

"I don't remember."

That seems to settle her, because she nods.

"I told him I was going to resign, and he was…well, he was furious. I'd never seen him so angry." I stare at her. "Maybe you're right. He considered it a sacred calling, maybe."

"You're far from a coward, Rem." She shakes her head.

"I know. He was angry. I was angry. I…regret that fight." It's the first time, maybe, that I've admitted that.

Regret quitting, even.

Because being back in the game has reawakened something inside me. Call it justice. Call it destiny.

Maybe it is a calling. Nevertheless, I owe Booker an apology.

I look away, out the window where the rain is lashing the pane. Lightning cracks, thunder rolls. And I know I sound a little crazy, but I can't stop myself from asking, "Did he leave me anything?"

I look back at Eve and of course she's frowning. "Uh, no. I mean…what?"

I sigh. "He had a watch. I was just wondering what happened

to it."

Eve shrugs. "You might want to ask Frankie." She gets up and heads back to the kitchen.

Frankie? I open my mouth, close it. Who is Frankie?

Except, in the next instant I'm remembering the odd conversation with the reporter today after Booker's funeral, aren't you?

"Why would Frankie know?" I follow Eve out and find her sitting at the counter, the foam container open, eating a wing. There's an open beer for me on the counter.

She puts down her half-eaten wing and grabs a napkin. "After her mom died, she got all his things, right? She probably donated most of them, but you could ask her."

I take a drink of the beer. Set it down. It holds no appeal for me anymore.

I look at her. "Why would Frankie have Booker's things?"

Eve is looking at me now, and I'm in trouble. "Are you okay, Rem?"

She has no idea how not okay I am.

"Frankie is Booker's daughter. Of course she'd get his things."

I sink down on a counter stool. Booker was never married in the worlds I knew.

"Honey, you're starting to scare me."

I go to the fridge and find a bottled water. Open it and drink it half down. If Frankie is Booker's daughter, then maybe she has the watch. It's at least a possibility, right?

My thought is interrupted by a flash, and the almost immediate crack of thunder. Eve jumps. "That sounded close."

Then a terrible crack rips through the air, cutting through the rain and thunder and a sudden, dark premonition makes me reach for Eve.

I take her to the floor under our big kitchen table just as the old elm crashes through our kitchen.

It's like a bomb has exploded, glass shattering, wood splintering, the implosion of tile and roofing shingles, electrical lines snapping, and behind it a roaring of thunder and rain.

Eve is clutching my shirt, burying her head against my chest and all I can do is hold onto her.

Just hold on.

Because this, my friends, is my life.

CHAPTER 6

There's a sort of insulation that happens when your life implodes around you. A shock that forms a barrier between your actions and the explosion of your emotions, as if, without your permission, the words form inside your head…"*I'll pick up those pieces later.*"

At least that's how I cope. Like when my brother Mickey went missing. I may have mentioned that he was with me that Saturday afternoon, and we were biking into town to go swimming at the lake.

I went around a corner, maybe a hundred yards ahead of him.

By the time I realized he wasn't behind me, by the time I turned back and retraced our route, found his bike in the weeds, he'd been taken.

Apparently, in this lifetime, John Booker found his murderer, shortly after the man dumped his body.

Meanwhile, I raced home, and my family spun up into action, alerting the police, neighbors and the community.

The insulation of activity.

I relish it now as I stand in the street, drenched by the rain as the firefighters extinguish the flames ignited by the sparking electrical lines severed by the giant elm tree dissecting our house.

Eve stands beside me, but I can still feel her in my embrace, shaking as the house collapsed around us as we huddled under the sturdy oak table handed down to us by my parents.

I hadn't noticed that until Eve pointed it out, as we extricated ourselves from the tangle of branches and debris. "Your parents' table saved us."

Her voice trembled, and I said nothing, intent on finding our way through the dark rubble of our home. Tangled and broken branches clawed at us, a war zone of destruction, the night still stinging us with rain as we crawled down the hallway, then to our front door.

It wasn't until I stumbled off the porch and onto the street that I saw the fire.

Old electrical lines, now broken, had lit the ancient insulation and ignited the garage roof.

Eve wove her fingers through mine a second before a voice sounded behind us.

"Are you guys okay?"

I turned and found, coming out of the house across the street, my neighbor, Alex. He's a good looking guy, short dark hair. A salesman, I think. Pharmaceuticals maybe. He's wearing a pair of jeans and a T-shirt. His wife, Gia, is behind him, a bathrobe thrown around her, her dark hair back.

So, they're still together in this timeline.

"We heard the tree. Called 911." He came up beside me, then. "Wow."

He's right. Even now, as the firefighters spray the fire—most of it consuming the garage contents, and dying with the rain, the place looks devastated. Not a clean hit, we'd say in football—the tree left a chaos of debris in its wake. The old roof is caved in over the garage and kitchen, my office probably also destroyed.

The front porch hangs from its foundation on one side as if trying to escape, and all the windows on the upper floor are shattered, probably from the force of the blow.

The elm was massive—probably eighty feet, with four or five thick branches.

Like I said, not a clean hit and I just hope I've kept up with my insurance payments.

See, like I said, insulation. But I need it as a wall caves in on the garage, as the firemen redirect their spray to the upper floors of the house, trying to save them.

I think the house is a goner.

Gia has come out with a couple umbrellas for us, but it's useless. In the meantime, she's talking to Russell, our other neighbor, an ex-NFL lineman turned lawyer. She's got her rain jacket pulled around her but is peering at him with something that looks a little too neighborly.

Alex is talking with one of the cops on the scene. I have a pretty clear memory, still, of a loud domestic fight between he and Gia a couple lifetimes ago.

Given the way his wife is looking at Russell, I think I know the reason why.

"It's a good thing we never started that remodel," Eve says, wrapping her arms around herself.

I look at her. She's drenched and shivering. I put my arm around her. "Why didn't we?"

She looks up at me. Shrugs, but I think there's an answer in her eyes. "It never felt like the right time." Maybe, but Eve has always been a remodeler, you know that, so there's something more.

A car pulls up, parks in the fog of a lamplight and a man gets out.

It's strange to see Danny Mulligan in the now. Strange… but good. That he's here proves that I haven't destroyed every life I've touched with this time travel business. He hasn't changed much—spare frame, still has a bit of a swagger when he walks. He's wearing a baseball hat, a raincoat and comes up to us with a grim look. "Got a call from dispatch," he says answering the question I didn't ask. "You guys okay?"

I nod, but Eve scoots over to him quick and gives a hug.

He holds her but looks over her head to me. "You can stay with us while you get back on your feet."

Admittedly, it does feel a little like I've lost my footing.

We stand there for another hour while the firemen put out the blaze in our home. The police tape it off and Eve and I are finally able to take a look inside.

In the shadows and smoke of the house, still dripping with water, the floors destroyed and soggy, I manage to break through to my office.

I hope I'm still smart and have backed up my files from my drenched computer to the cloud. But what I want, what I *need*, is the box.

The cold case files.

Just in case this world isn't permanent.

I dig out the box, and then head upstairs to our bedroom.

The window has been blown out, and although the carpet is saturated, the furniture is still intact.

Eve has piled some clothes and toiletries in a couple pillow cases near the door. But she's not in the room.

I find her down the hall, in the empty room that in a different lifetime, was pink and filled with stuffed animals and horses. And the laughter of my … I yank myself out of a thousand memories and focus back on Eve.

She's opened the closet door and is wrestling out a box. I go to help her. "What's this?"

She looks at me and frowns. "What do think it is? It's Ashley's box. I just…" She takes a breath. "I just don't want to leave it behind."

Ashley's box.

It's like she's put a fist through my chest, but I manage to breathe through the wound and lift it into my arms. "Of course."

I carry it down the stairs and add it to my cold case files. I guess they belong together.

Then I retrieve the pillowcases with our worldly belongings and join Eve in the foyer. She's holding a satchel stuffed with what looks like pictures. She offers me a brave smile.

I'm dying to know what happened to Ashley, but the truth is, I'm too afraid to ask. And not just because how Eve will react, but what if it's something I can't change?

If you haven't guessed it by now, the truth is I'm hoping I can find the watch. That Booker has left it in Frankie's hands.

At least then I'd have options.

I could go back, cut down the tree, stop Leo and maybe even save Booker's life.

My list is getting complicated.

Danny is waiting on the porch and I hand him the pillowcases, then go back for the boxes and we trek out to his car.

The house is forlorn and dark as we leave, the sky still spitting on us.

Danny and Bets Mulligan live in the suburbs, in a little community on the lake in a farmhouse Bets inherited from her family. The place is over a hundred years old but was updated when Bets took a sledgehammer to her kitchen wall. Now the former galley kitchen opens up to a massive great room that overlooks the lake.

Tonight, the lake is angry, waves frothing on the shoreline as I stand at the window of Eve's upstairs bedroom.

We're sleeping in her childhood double bed, which feels weird, right? But it's safe and dry, a bastion in the storm, so to speak.

She's showered, changed into dry clothes and is curled under the blankets, quiet.

Not asleep.

I've showered too, but I still feel grimy, frayed and rattled.

The insulation is wearing off.

"I should have cut down that tree," I say, more to myself, the list of woulda-coulda-shouldas cluttering my brain.

"You were going to put a swing on it," Eve says.

I glance at her. Yes, I was. But then a storm, not unlike this one, broke off a branch and I realized the danger of such a large tree near our house.

I'm not sure why I wasn't paying attention this time around.

I'm starting to think that no matter what I do, what timeline I'm in, how many times I go back to fix my past, I'm going to forget something.

Screw up something.

It's like that game in the arcade, the one with the moles. Only my version is Whack-A-Rem. And I'm not sure it's possible to win.

"Come to bed, love," she says. "I need you."

And of course, that's exactly the words that stop the clutter in my brain. I crawl in beside her and tuck her body next to mine, spooning.

She takes my hand and holds it close. "We lived. That's the important part. That's enough."

Yes, I guess it is.

Maybe it's the exhaustion that makes me sleep, or Eve's

warmth, but I tumble into sweet oblivion.

I land hard, however, in the middle of a familiar dream. You know the one—I'm on the ice in the middle of a lake. It's the dead of winter, everything crisp and brown, cattails and marshland that edges the lake stiff under the brutal cold.

I can nearly feel it too—the cold that seeps into my pores, turns my body frozen. I'm shivering.

The ice is clear, thick and scarred with the carcasses of birds and branches caught in the freeze. A slight wind bullies the snow off it, catching in my eyes. They water.

And the wind. It's moaning, a deep howl behind me, as if gathering.

In it, I hear a voice. *Rembrandt.*

I feel I know that voice, but I can't place it as I stand there, the wind filling my ears.

It's then I hear a gunshot. A sharp report that scatters birds, spears the air.

Beneath my feet, a fissure has opened. I look down and the crack is webbing out.

Run.

I scrabble over the ice toward shore, my rubber boots slipping, and I fall.

I catch myself on the ice with familiar red mittens. The ice spiders out in fractures under my grip. I scramble to my feet and keep running. But the shoreline has slipped away, reset.

I'm further than when I started. My breathing is labored now, and as the ice opens behind me, the water black and lethal, I am screaming.

Help!

Because I know if I don't keep running, the water will find me. Pull me under.

I'll disappear and never be found.

"Rem!"

The voice lifts from the shore and I thrash around, trying to find it.

"Rembrandt!"

I've fallen again, bracing myself on the ice, and look back.

The ice breaks open beneath me, and—

"Rem, wake up!"

The voice, a hand on my arm frees me and I gasp awake, my heart thundering, a cold sweat sheeting my body.

Eve is leaning over me, one elbow on the narrow mattress. "You're dreaming."

I press a fist to my forehead and stare at the ceiling. A thin shadow of golden-red light streaks across the ceiling through the blinds.

"Which dream was it?"

I look over at her. "The ice."

She nods. "The one where you never get to shore."

So, my demons are at least consistent across timelines in their torment.

"Go back to sleep," I say and roll over and kiss her cheek. Then I get up because my body is edgy and rattled. And, frankly, I'd like to do something more than sleep in my bed, but Eve looks wrung out.

And we're in her parents' home, right?

So, I get up and pull on a pair of jeans and a T-shirt and head downstairs in search of coffee.

I'm quiet, and I make a pot of French press, then take my cup out to the family room, standing at the big picture window.

The wreckage of last night's storm litters the formerly manicured lawn. Hosta leaves shredded and cast about the yard, twigs down from the arching cottonwood beside the house, and froth from the lake edging the tattered beach. The dock looks intact, however, the boat up from the water.

Overhead, the sunrise bleeds deep burnt orange over the lake and lighting the sky in an array of light blue, deep orange and fiery red.

Breathtaking, really.

"It's always a sort of miracle to me how beautiful the sunrise is after a storm." Bets comes up beside me, a sweater wrapped around her, her reddish-blonde hair pulled back in a handkerchief. "It's like the chaos of the night congeals to form this beautiful fresh start."

That's what I need. A fresh start out of all this clutter.

The sense that it's not in vain.

"I can still remember waking up after surgery. I was hurting and scared and confused—and then I saw Danny's face. He was standing there, just broken. He'd been crying—he never cries, but…he was scared, I guess."

We were all scared. I don't tell her that the first time around, Danny was the one that was shot. It doesn't matter anymore, really.

"Funny thing was, I was always afraid of Danny getting a bullet through him on the job. The last thing I thought was that I'd get shot."

Um, and that's my fault, too, if we're honest. I take a sip of my coffee. It's hot and bracing and exactly what my bones need.

Everybody lived. That's what's important.

"And I realized I'd lived my entire life afraid of what-ifs. But the what-if had *just happened*, and I came out the other side. And yes, it hurt, and I'm so glad it wasn't Danny who was shot, but… each day is a gift, right? And if I live in fear of that what-ifs, it just leaches the happiness out of what I do have."

She has poured herself a cup of coffee and now takes a sip.

Watches the sun as it turns the lake to crimson. "There will always be storms, Rem. But we can't live in fear of them. We weather them. We get stronger. And then we get back up and go on in the beauty of a new sunrise."

I don't know. "So much meaningless destruction."

I guess I say that out loud because she pats my arm. "Is it, though? Because my starter is ready and I'm making sourdough pancakes."

She winks and heads to the kitchen, and I hear banging behind me, the clatter of pots and pans.

Danny appears in a moment, grabbing a cup of coffee, putting on fresh water for another batch and joins me in the family room, holding his phone. "Looks like a tornado touched down southwest of here, in a town about sixty miles away." He looks up at me. "I guess it could always be worse."

Huh. And that's when Eve comes down the stairs. She's wearing yoga pants, one of my old T-shirts, her hair down and kinky and when she looks at me, a soft smile on her lips, I know I should have stayed in bed.

But yes, Danny, it could have been much worse.

Bets is plating pancakes, and the smell of bacon rises in the air. Eve steals a piece, as the front door opens and in walks Sams, Eve's brother.

Sams is a real estate developer, but in his early days, he was a remodeler. He's tall and with golden blond hair and wide-shouldered and he grins at me like we don't have a past.

Hmm. Maybe in this world, we don't.

"I hear you guys might have a job for me." He also steals a piece of bacon. He gives Eve a one-armed hug, code for, *I'm glad you're all right.*

"Maybe I'll finally get that kitchen I've always wanted," she says.

I know it's a jab but I gave her that kitchen once-upon-a time. And, apparently, I will again.

Maybe Bets is right. *If I live in fear of that what-ifs, it just leaches the happiness out of what I do have.*

Bets serves me up a plate of pancakes, sizzling bacon and a glass of orange juice on her counter. "Come eat, Rem."

Such a simple statement, but that's it, isn't it? I slide onto the counter chair feeling oddly like I'm climbing out of the clutter into a new day.

Maybe fate is done wrestling with me.

Maybe it's time to let go.

I pour syrup over the pancakes, pick up my knife and I'm about to dig in when my cell phone vibrates in my jeans pocket. I fish it out and look at the screen. Frankie Dale. Her name is plugged into my contacts.

Huh. "Rembrandt here."

A breath on the other end of the line, a gulp and I put down my fork. "What's going on?"

"Rem, it's...it's Zeke."

I recognize her voice from yesterday, maybe, but I'm scrambling to put pieces together. Zeke knows Booker's daughter?

I still can't believe Booker has a *daughter*.

And I'm in the game. "Frankie, take a breath. What's going on?"

She seems to respond, her breaths evening out. "Zeke was shot."

"What? When?"

"This morning. Early. He was...he was coming home and someone was waiting for him, they think. He was shot just as he was getting out of his car."

His *Porsche.*

And a fist forms in my gut. Because you know what I said.

He reminds me of me.

And if he reminds me of me…maybe he reminds someone else of me, right?

Maybe not, but I've lost my appetite. "We're on our way."

The clutter is gone from my mind.

I'm on the job.

CHAPTER 7

This is personal. I know that sounds crazy, but fate and I are in a war, and I don't know about you, but to me, it feels like fate is up on the scoreboard.

Maybe it will win, but now I'm hot, laser focused and ready to launch myself back into the game.

I'm standing in Zeke's hospital room, my arms folded as he recounts his story to me and Eve. The morning has cleared to a blue sky, and crews are out on the streets cleaning up.

We dropped Sams off at the house on the way to the hospital, and he's going to meet the insurance investigator there, take a look at the foundation.

It looked worse in the morning, a woman the day after, her makeup smudged, her dress askew, trying to hide in the morning light. The garage and half the house are blackened, the rest smoke damaged. The tree lays across it, broken into pieces, a wounded villain.

Sorry, old tree. Somehow, I can't escape the idea that this is my fault.

Again.

I'm hoping we don't have to raze the house to the ground, but frankly, if that's what we have to do to rebuild my life, I'm ready.

Raze it all to the ground and start over.

"So where were you so early in the morning?" I say to Zeke, not quite clear on that part. "The gym?"

Frankie looks at me. Her eyes are puffy and red, like she's been crying. Her brown hair is down and long and she's wearing a pair of exercise pants, jogging shoes and a T-shirt.

I'm a jerk for the way I treated her in my office, but I can't exactly say why, so I smile at her.

No wonder I recognized her. She has Booker's dark, intelligent eyes, his nose, his wide mouth. Fact is, the reporter is a younger, female spitting image of him. She has his fiber, too, because her eyes hold no apology as she says, "My house."

Oh, I see. She's holding Zeke's hand, her thumb running over his. It feels oddly familiar to see them together like this, and the strangest flash of memory kicks in.

Me, at the hospital, Eve by my bedside, her hand in mine. And where and when it happened, I'm not sure, but I have a feeling it's from my stab wound, back when I took down Ramses.

Weird that those memories, the ones I don't remember living, are embedded inside me, as if part of my soul.

Meggie Fox called my time travel a type of chronothesis, a projection of myself back into my memories.

It's possible the new memories I created are merging with the old, maybe even overwriting them.

I will refuse to panic, but even as I think it, I try to conjure up a memory of Ashley. My Ash, with the long blonde braids. She smiles back at me, her blue eyes bright and a wash of relief slips through me.

We're okay. She's still there.

"You see the person who shot you?" I ask Zeke, without comment on Frankie's answer.

Zeke looks rough. He's been shot in the shoulder, the bullet breaking his collarbone, just missing his lung.

Lucky.

But when he fell, he broke his nose, and, like he's the loser of a brawl, his nose is purple, his eyes puffy with blood.

"Not really. It happened so fast. I just parked my car and was walking behind it to my place when a car pulled up and someone just shot me. No hesitation, as if he knew what he was doing."

"You don't remember—"

"I was looking at my phone."

Right. No one looks out at the world anymore. A whole generation with their noses buried in the internet.

"Okay, take a breath. I'm just trying to think of who might want to hurt you. What cases are you working?"

He lifts his good shoulder, then winces. "The Jackson case, mostly. I've been working Hollie Larue's murder—tracking down witnesses, talking to her friends."

"Anything else?" I ask.

"Just…I guess looking into the bombing, you know."

Of my *Porsche*. "Malakov's gang."

"You think this could be an attack?" Eve asks. She didn't pack work clothes and is wearing a T-shirt and jeans. Her hair is up, however, her black-rimmed glasses perched on her nose

I've never seen them before—she had Lasik surgery years ago. I find the glasses quite fetching.

Her gaze on me, not so much. "I don't know, Eve."

She winds her hands around her waist. "Silas and his team are at the scene. We'll know more when they're finished."

There's at least one more person they haven't mentioned.

"What about Ramses Vega?"

Zeke shakes his head. "I've been rolling by his house every day, just like you asked. I think I would have recognized him." He sighs. "Or maybe not. I just remember the shooter wore a baseball cap, and a pair of sunglasses, and he shot me with his left hand."

His left hand. That's interesting.

Maybe Eve thinks so too because she's frowning. "I can check his files. Sometimes they list it, sometimes they don't."

"I'll make this easy and ask Mayor Vega." I reach for my phone but Eve touches my arm.

"Maybe let me. The last thing you need is for Vega to hate you more."

I sigh, but maybe she's right.

Besides, in my gut, I don't think it was Vega, do you?

Malakov's gang, maybe, but even that doesn't feel right.

I know exactly what happened, and it fills me like a poison.

"What about Fitzgerald?" I ask, and I keep my voice casual, not at all like a grenade.

It doesn't work. "You think Leo Fitzgerald could have done this?" Frankie says, her eyes widening. "Because Zeke got too close?"

"It doesn't fit his M.O.," Eve says, but she looks at me and I wonder if she's remembering what Gunter said. *"He's made this personal."*

Maybe he thought Zeke was me. In fact, I'm nearly sure of it.

"Why haven't we caught this guy?" My voice comes out more like a growl and I walk to the window, staring out at the skyline. "How is it that Leo Fitzgerald has eluded us for over *twenty* years?"

There's silence behind me, and when I turn, no one is looking at me. "Really? With all we have on this guy? His address? His DNA? His MO. His tattoo?"

I turn to Eve. "I even have a picture of the guy, from the photo you grabbed from Midtown Ink."

In case you're wondering, Fitzgerald is over six feet, bearded, hair clipped short, a tattoo on his upper forearm. The tat is of two hands, gripping each other, wrapped in barbed wire that also encircles the upper arm. The word BRO is inked on a ribbon that winds through the art.

We got his ink from the photo of a partial tattoo caught by a parking garage camera after we found victim twenty-two. It's what I used to track down Leo, twenty-four years prior, in Montrose.

Where we had our little scuffle.

"Good memory," Eve says.

"Did we ever talk to his buddies? The guys from the Big Red One, first infantry? From Desert Storm?"

"Yes. No one has seen him for years," Zeke says.

"And, we don't have his address, Rem," Eve says quietly.

I stare at her. But maybe not—after all, the only address I remember is the one involved in Booker's ambush.

Which, in this timeline, never happened.

Unfortunately, I didn't memorize it, not realizing I needed it.

Believing I could change time.

I sigh. "What about his military records?"

"His mother had a place here, but she sold it years ago."

Perfect.

"So, the guy is in the wind, and we have nothing?"

Eve lifts her shoulder.

I meet her eyes. "Okay, this is going to sound crazy, but I need you to trust me."

She nods.

"I need you to pull the files of the people who survived the CityPerk bombing back in 1997."

She frowns. "Rem, what do you mean survived? We all survived. You stopped it."

"I meant witnessed the *attempted* attack." I meet her gaze. "I realize it's out of your purview, but I need help."

"Okay," she says quietly.

"I need to know if Leo Fitzgerald was one of the people in the coffee shop that day. If he was, the report should have a home address for him. We can start there."

She's still frowning. "Is this one of your crazy hunches?"

"It's not crazy if it works." I get up. "We're going to build a fresh profile for this guy. We're going to start by looking at every single victim. Figure out what they have in common. It's not about motive, means, and opportunity anymore. We're looking at what happened and asking *why* it happened this way. We're going to get inside his head and figure out how this guy hunts."

My word *hunt* has shut down the room, but like I said, the clutter is gone.

If I'm stuck here, I'm going to find Leo Fitzgerald in the here and now.

I turn to Frankie. "I want you to write down everything I tell you. And then publish it in tomorrow's paper."

"Is this an exclusive?"

"From the chief of police, yes."

She is smiling and digs out her phone. "Can I tape you?"

"You bet. Let's start with this. There's a killer out there. And he's targeting women between the ages of eighteen and thirty, people who work in the service industry—waitresses, bartenders, working girls. Our best guess is that he waits for his victims after work, follows them and runs them down. Then he strangles them."

Frankie's eyes are wide, and I realize I've scared her. So, I add, "I'm telling every woman who works in one of these professions to not travel alone, not close up late by themselves, to carry pepper spray and if you're afraid, call the police and ask for an escort."

"What does he look like?"

I give her the description I know.

She looks at me. "Do you think this will help?"

Zeke takes her hand. "It's okay. Rem will capture him." Then he grins at me.

Eve's right. It's exactly how I used to look at John Booker.

Frankie stops the recording. "You remind me a little of John when you get like this. He would get this look in his eye when he was onto something..." She rubs her thumb over the phone. "It's one of my most vivid memories of him."

I can't help it. "Frankie, I'm so sorry, I can't remember. How old were you when John died?"

"I was six."

Wow. But I'm still confused. "I don't understand. Why do you call him John, and not—"

"Dad?"

I raise a shoulder, and I can feel Eve's eyes on me, as if we've had this conversation, but I'm going to ignore her.

"Because my dad was Henry Dale, the man who raised me. John Booker was...well, my mom and he probably should have never gotten married. They both admit that. But he was a good man. Supported me, came around a lot. I thought of him more as an uncle than a father. He loved me, though."

I wish with everything inside me, I could remember Frankie in John's life. And how it's possible he had a daughter I didn't know about.

See, he's in the past, mucking it all up.

"Did he..." It's long shot, I know, but, "Did John leave you his watch?"

She frowns, then shakes her head. "I think he might have been buried with it."

The words are dropped so causally, but they have the effect of a bomb exploding in my brain. *Booker was buried with the watch.*

I want to press my hand to my chest, to see if my heart is still beating.

A knock sounds at the door and Burke pokes his head in. "Hey. I heard you were taking up bed space here," he says to Zeke.

Zeke grins, although it's more of a twisted grimace given his injuries. Burke walks in and he's carrying a cup of coffee. "We're on our way home, but I thought I'd stop by."

"How's Shelby?" Eve asks.

"Tired, but good."

"And Daphne?"

Burke grins. "Beautiful."

There's an ache deep inside, but I ignore it.

"So, who did you tick off?" Burke says, but I see the concern he's trying to hide.

"Dunno," Zeke says. "Rembrandt thinks it's Fitzgerald."

Burke looks over at me.

Thanks, Zeke, but I don't care. "You heard about the bodies in the field, right?"

He nods.

"The backyard of my *parents'* home."

He looks at his coffee.

"He might be in my head, but I'm clearly in his, too," I say. "Why?"

"Maybe it's because you beat the tar out of him twenty-odd years ago," Burke says.

I shake my head. "This guy is military. And he *won*. He got away." I look at Eve. "This guy is about power, like Gunter said.

He's likes to win."

"Gunter says he's playing a game with you."

"Again, why me? Why am I special to him now?"

Burke looks at me, his gaze even. "Now, you're the police chief. It can't be a coincidence that the day you take the position is the day the tip is called in."

I consider his words. But they don't make sense. "I wasn't supposed to take the job for at least another week. Shelby went into labor early."

I look at Frankie. "But you know what was scheduled for yesterday?"

"John's commemorative ceremony," she says.

I nod. "So what was I doing before John was killed that would make Leo want me to remember that date?"

"Check your journal. You probably wrote about it."

My…*journal.*

The word takes a sweep through me.

Good, good job young me, listening to your elders.

Burke turns to Zeke. "You'll be fine, buck. A little PT with Gene Latsky and he'll get you back in one piece." He glances at me. "He fixed Rem up, and then me. And didn't he help your mom, too, Eve?"

She nods, but I'm blank.

Who is Gene?

I have a faint memory, although foggy. A guy at a bar. Blond hair. Big hands. *Keep up those stretches. The scar tissue can tighten up, and pretty soon your muscles are all knotted."*

"Gene is our physical therapist," I say, a sort of realization.

Burke's eyebrow dips down, but he nods.

"He knows Leo Fitzgerald," I say softly.

The room goes quiet. I'm nodding. "He was playing pool with

him the day Leo and I got into it at the bar in Montrose."

Burke is staring at me. "Are you sure? That was a long time ago."

Sure. To some people. *I* remember it like it happened forty-eight hours ago.

"I'm sure."

Burke takes a sip of his coffee. "That might have been helpful information."

I hear the reprimand, but I don't care.

I'm smiling.

Because this round against fate belongs to me.

CHAPTER 8

I have a foggy memory of Gene Latsky. There's enough of a bookmark to know I've met him, and when, but that's the extent of the imprint.

I'm hoping hard that he has a better memory than I do.

I track him down at the University of Minnesota physical therapy department. The hospital is clean, quiet and his office is in the rehabilitation clinic on the third floor. I stand in the lobby and watch the row team fighting the current of the Mississippi River. The river is dark, frothy and flowing high today after last night's storm.

Strong arms, packed with youth, but they're not making much headway against the power of the river.

"Rembrandt Stone. How you are?" Gene Latsky isn't a remarkable person. Tall, over six feet, a little paunch, thinning blonde hair, blue eyes and he has a strong handshake. He's wearing a lightweight long-sleeve shirt, a pair of cargo pants and tennis shoes and greets me with a smile.

Because of course, he knows *me*.

"Hey Gene," I say, like we saw each other a few days ago.

Because, you know, we *did*. "How are you?"

"Good, good, good. Yeah. And you? How's that shoulder?"

Shoulder. Not a clue of what he's talking about, but I nod.

"That's the spirit. Old gunshot wounds are likely to bind up with age, so keep working that muscle."

"I'll bear that in mind."

He leads me back, into his office, and when we get inside, I see a number of plaques and awards on his wall, a clutter of old pictures—a football team, a shot of young him in a military uniform, along with a shelf of books. My gaze lands on a familiar book. "You've got my memoir, *The Last Year*." I walk over and pick it up.

I wrote the book during my rookie year as an investigator. It got picked up by a publisher and somehow turned into a New York Times best-seller.

It's what paid for my Porsche, may she rest in peace.

"Did you forget that you gave it to me?" He takes it and flips open the cover. "To Gene. No matter how much it hurts, I'll always be back." He's grinning, and reshelves the book.

"After I was stabbed," I say, remembering our conversation from the bar.

"Yeah. As I remember you were working on a second book. A novel?"

Interesting. So once a writer, always a writer, regardless of the timelines. "Yes. It's still up here." I tap my head.

He laughs. "That's what you said last time, too. You need me to look at your shoulder?" He indicates one of his chairs.

I don't sit. "No. I just need to ask you a question." I take a breath. "I don't know if you remember this, but many years ago, I came into a bar in Montrose, looking for a suspect, and you were there."

He folds his arms, nods. "Of course I remember. You got into a scrap with the guy I was playing pool with." He's wearing a smirk. "If I remember right, he owned you."

"Thanks for that."

"Aw." He gives me a slap on the arm. "Shake it off."

"Did you know him?"

He drops his hand. Frowns. "Not really. He was in the military, and that made him a bro, but that's all."

Hmm. "You sure? You two looked pretty friendly."

He makes a face, shakes his head. "Naw. He just liked shooting stick. I live out that way, and like to go over to the Joint to work off the day, right?" He lifts a shoulder.

"Remember his name?"

"Lenny, maybe?"

Hmm. "Seen him around since?"

"In the last twenty years? Uh, sure. Yeah. I don't know."

"Recently?"

He frowns again. Deeper this time. "What's this about?"

I run a hand over my mouth, then walk to the window. The rowers are still fighting the current, having made little headway. "He's a suspect in a murder case."

Gene is quiet behind me. Then, "Who did he kill?"

I don't know where to start, but one answer stands out. "A little girl."

He makes a noise, something of a groan. "That's horrible."

"It is." I glance at him.

He's giving me a strange look. "And this crime—it happened twenty years ago?"

"It started twenty-four years ago. But he's still at large."

"Still murdering little girls?"

I nod, because it's close enough. "I need to find him and stop him."

"Yes, you do." He walks up next to me. "The one that just keeps getting away."

I say nothing.

"That's a long game to play with someone."

I think he's calling me obsessed.

Gene is watching the rowers too. "There's this phenomenon we have in the industry called a phantom pain. It's a pain that happens in a limb that is perceived, even after the limb is gone. Sometimes it helps to play a trick on the mind—to put a mirror to the remaining limb, making it seem like the missing limb is there. The brain can then interact with the missing limb. Scratch it, or unclench a fist, or even just move it."

I don't understand.

"For a little while, then, the pain abates. But then, the mind realizes it's been tricked, and it returns and they're back in my office with the same wound, looking for more treatment."

"Are you saying that I'm looking for him to help soothe some inner wound?" I clench my jaws. "He's a killer. I'm doing my job."

"I'm saying when the body perceives an emptiness, it reaches out in pain until something can replace it."

I stare at him.

"Ashley," he says quietly. "Maybe your job helps fill the emptiness."

I can't breathe. "How do you know about my daughter?"

He frowns. "I was at her funeral."

Right. Everyone but me.

"This isn't about my daughter," I say. "But yes, there isn't a day that goes by that I don't think about her." I don't know why but saying that loosens a clench in my chest.

Missing Ashley has become a phantom pain, because no one understands the depth of what I've lost.

I'm still holding onto her. Unfortunately, no mirror is going to bring her back. Ease the grip of grief. That thought hits me as I turn to him.

I have rewritten the one person I can't replace. And no matter how many times I go back, she is gone.

"Think you'll find him?" he asks quietly and meets my eyes.

I can't place the look. Maybe it's just a polite question. Maybe it's worry. I don't know, but I meet his gaze. "Yeah. Yeah, I will. He'll make a mistake, and when he does, I will be there."

He draws in a breath. Then smiles. "I'm sure you will."

"If you can think of anything, let me know, okay?"

"You got it, Chief." He holds out his hand, smiling. "For what it's worth, I'm glad you didn't quit."

I grip his hand a little longer than normal. And a little tighter.

He frowns. "Don't tell me you don't remember. Right after you got shot. You and Jimmy Williams. The way he tells it, you took a bullet for him."

"I was just in the right place the right time," I say, making a mental note to look that up.

"I thought for sure you were going to quit the force. You sounded so sure, so ready to be done. And then Ashley died."

I still.

"And I guess that kept you in the game, right?" He clamps me on the shoulder again. "Gotta fill those gaps."

"Right," I manage.

I head downtown and stop by the coffee kiosk on my way through to my office. But I stop in the lobby and change directions, and head upstairs to the mayor's office.

I can admit, I have a burr under my skin.

Her secretary rises when she sees me. "She's requested no visitors."

"Perfect. Then we can have a private chat." And I walk into her office.

Mariana has her shoes off and is drinking a green smoothie while watching the news on her flatscreen. Picking up the remote, she clicks it to mute, but doesn't get up. "What?"

"Where was your son this morning, around six a.m.?"

"Why?" She pulls her bare feet off her coffee table and leans forward.

"One of my officers was shot."

She shakes her head. "Ramses was home, with me."

I press my lips together, want to call her a liar, but who knows? "Is your son right-handed?"

She frowns. "Why?"

"Just answer the question."

She takes a drink of her smoothie through a straw. "Ramses didn't shoot anyone. Go away."

I stand there a moment, then, "The second he doesn't check in with his parole officer, I'm on him, Vega."

"That's Mayor Vega, Acting Chief Stone." She's set down her drink. "And next time you want to talk to me, make an appointment."

She picks up her remote and turns on the volume. I turn back to the door, but I hear a sigh from behind me, as the volume clicks back off again.

"How is your officer, Acting Chief Stone?"

"He's still alive."

Her voice is almost conciliatory as she looks me in the eye. "I'm telling you the truth. He was with me last night. And if I thought Ramses was capable of this, I would tell you."

Sure. "Would you?" I turn and leave quickly. That's my charm quota for the day.

Reagan, my assistant rises from his desk as I stride into my office area. "Your brother-in-law called here."

I dig into my pocket and discover my cell has died. That's what happens when you leave your charger in the middle of a soggy house.

"I have an extra cord," Reagan says and hands me a coil from his desk.

I like this guy. On the ball. "Thanks."

I plug in my phone. Then I use the office phone and call Sams.

"Hey," he says. "The tree removal crew is here. I also walked through the house with the insurance guy. He says that most of the house will need to be taken down. If you want, I can get a crew in here tomorrow—"

"Wait—" I take a breath. And I know what I said about starting over, but— "I need to talk to Eve."

And I need to get in the house. Remember what Eve said about my journal? If I'm grubbing around for clues from the past, I should probably start with my own brain.

"Okay. Get over here when you can. I'll stick around."

"Thanks, Sams." I hang up and boot up my phone.

I'm hoping the man I'm looking for is still around. Still has his ear to the ground of the underworld.

I find Yasir Isse's number in my contacts and hold my breath a little as the line rings.

Someone picks up. "Seriously?"

Bingo. "Yasir?"

"Inspector. Why are you calling me?"

I wish I knew how long it's been since we last talked, but I'm taking a chance that I've stayed connected with the man who helped me find his sister-in-law's kids and save their lives.

"I need some information. There's word on the street that a

Russian gang under the leadership of a guy named Sergei Malakov has declared war on my police department."

"And what would I know about this?"

I pause. Because it's a good question. But in my silence, he says, "Go on."

Not all my hunches are from the future. I was a good investigator, once upon a time.

"I need a name. Someone who might have information on the Malakov gang."

"Why?"

"Because cops are getting shot." It feels like an easy answer.

"I'll sniff around. Maybe then you'll leave me alone."

"Unlikely," I say. "Thanks, Yasir."

He hangs up, I grab my coffee and head up to Eve's office.

I find her standing at the window, looking out at a clear blue, almost pale sky, not a hint of storm in the wispy clouds. "You okay?"

She looks at me. Nods. "I feel like my life is unraveling."

I put my coffee down and pull her against me. "We'll rebuild, Eve."

She wraps her arms around me. "I'm living in limbo land. I don't like it."

"Let's focus on finding our serial killer." I step away. "Did you pull the CityPerk file?"

She nods, picking up her glasses and walking over to the board. "I have a list of three names. I don't know that they'll help."

I open the file and scan the names. I remember them. The barista, Katia Higgins, her son, Noel, and a lawyer, Graham Morris. All of them tell the same story—the one where Burke and I corner Ramses Vega and take him down right after he left the bomb under the counter. "Do we know where these people are today?"

"Katia Higgins is still the owner slash barista of CityPerk, and her son, Noel is helping her run it." She walks over to a board where I see she's put up pictures. "Graham Morris now lives in Chicago, and is a partner at Morris, Simmons and Seay."

I can't help being a bit disappointed. Except—the last time around, the blast destroyed the entire city block. "Do you have names of people who were in the surrounding buildings?"

"I still don't know how you knew the bomber would be there." She walks over to the board, and studies the faces and names pinned onto it. "You'll have to check the notes on the bystanders."

"I made a list of the all the victims, too, trying to find similarities." She gestures to the board. "Aside from all the markers—the strangulation, the sexual assault, the twenty-dollar bill—they come from all demographics. There's no economic baseline, no geography similarities. The only consistent profile is that all the victims are white, all in service industries, and all of them were killed after their shift, late at night."

She steps back from the board. "According to Gunter, our guy is an organized killer. Which means he probably knows them, even stalks them beforehand. So, how does he choose them?"

"That's the link," I say.

Her desk phone rings and she picks it up. "Sams."

"We'd better get over there."

She picks up her satchel, puts it over her shoulder and reaches inside.

And pulls out the pictures she's taken from the house.

She sets one on the desk.

It's a blow to my chest, but I manage not to gasp. Ashley, age four, on a swing, me next to her. I'm grinning, my eyes shining, and I don't remember ever being this happy.

Maybe I do, but it's a faded memory.

Crazily, my eyes burn.

Eve slides her hand into mine. "Ever think about how our lives would be different if Ashley had lived?"

I can barely answer her. "Every day, Eve. Every single day."

She looks at me, but I squeeze her hand. "Let's go."

One thing is clear.

If I want to solve this, I need to get to my house, before it turns to rubble.

CHAPTER 9

I know without a doubt that I would have written the details of my daughter's murder in my journal. And this is the only thing tempering Eve's words about Ashley, roaming raw and untended in my brain. *Ever think about how our lives would be different if she hadn't been murdered?*

Please let the journal have answers. Because the longer I stick around, the more I haven't a clue what I'm doing. It's like showing up late to a movie.

A crane is parked in the middle of my street as we pull up in Eve's father's truck. (Our Ford Escape is currently a burned-out hull in our garage.)

A tree removal service has already severed the arms of the tree and the crane is removing the massive trunk in pieces.

A woodchipper grinds up the debris and is shooting it into a truck.

I'm not sure why the rattle of the machine grates on me as I get out, but it's loud and violent and the sight of my ravaged house doesn't help my mood.

The tree removal service has roped off the area, but I'm heading toward the house when a hand on my arm stops me. "Whoa, there, Rem. You trying to get yourself killed?"

Sams. He's a big guy, and I know he can handle himself, so I don't really want to get into it with him, but I am going in my house, thank you.

"I need to get in there," I say.

Sams pulls me back, though and points to the crane overhead, which is hauling a tree across the very spot I just stood. "Just trying to keep you from getting pancaked."

Most of the tree is off the front part of the house, just the debris of the leaves left to clutter the demolished porch. "When will they finish?"

He shrugs "Tomorrow?"

I nod and head over to the crane operator. "Hey!"

He's the usual tough. He wears a gimme cap, a T-shirt and leans out the window, one beefy hand on the door. "Get back!"

"That's my house. I have to get in."

He frowns. There are a half-dozen other guys working the area—picking up branches, using chainsaws. A couple of them look over at me.

"Can you take a break?"

Crane man considers me a minute, then nods, and shuts off the crane. "Take fifteen, guys!"

I'm not sure what convinced him—maybe I'm wearing something desperate in my expression. But as he climbs down, I head toward the ruins of my home.

"I'm going with you!" Eve says as she runs up to me. I catch her arms. "Hon. I just need my journal." And then, "Do you remember where I keep it?"

She frowns at me, and I deserve that, but I'm going to have to take a chance. "In your office desk."

Right.

"Be careful, Rem."

I mouth, "I will" and approach the steps. The front porch is precariously perched on the ancient foundation, and I tread carefully as I head inside. The place is dark, soggy and smells of smoke. It's a good thing Eve stayed outside. The insurance man is right—it might be easier to take it down to the foundation.

My office is at the front of the house, and still intact, although my awards have been knocked off the shelf by the power of the fire hose, and my desk is puckered. My computer is, of course, dead, the carpet soggy.

But as I pull out my desk drawer, I see it there, on the top—the fat composition book I gave myself twenty-four years ago. The edges are worn, and as I open it, I see my handwriting. Dates, details of crime scenes, my investigations and, hopefully, enough information to fill in the swiss cheese memory of my life.

I'm turning to go when I spot a picture I don't recognize.

It's my dad and me. I'm about seventeen, and I'm standing on the ice, bundled up, holding a stringer of fish. We're grinning.

I pick it up and just like that, almost with a whoosh, I'm there, back in the memory.

The lake is frozen, just like in my dream, but we're sitting in an ice house, drinking hot cocoa, and my dad is telling my Uncle Bert a story. I don't remember the words, but I do remember the sound of my father's laughter. It's like a summer wind, fresh and unexpected.

Booker told me once that time travel was a gift. A way to give people closure. To let them live in peace.

I didn't believe him then, thinking I could do better.

I was so arrogant back then. All of two weeks ago.

Grabbing the picture, I tiptoe back out of the house.

Crane man is standing by his truck. I lift my hand.

He nods and gets back in.

Eve and I stand on the street for a while, watching. "It's just a house," she says.

Not on your life. But I say nothing as we finally drive to the Mulligans.

Eve is quiet and I look over at her as we pull into the drive. "You okay?"

"I'm not sure," she says and looks at me. "I hope so."

I frown, but we go inside to the smell of pot roast and baked potatoes. Bets is old school, and I've never left their house without a solid meal in my gullet. Still, my brain is busy, and I'm feeling edgy. Although I want to dive into the journal immediately, I instead change into a pair of shorts, a shirt and running shoes and take off for a run before dinner.

I'm not sure why, but I think reading the journal will make me feel a little like a voyeur, looking back into my past. Like the voice won't belong to me, but a different version of myself.

Someone I don't really know.

I turn my headphones onto my favorite radio station and take off at a fast clip, heading down the road past the mansions that border the lake. This part of town is more modest—older homes built in the fifties and sixties when lake property was still affordable. I pass groomed lawns, sprinklers awakening in the late afternoon. The sun will still be up for hours, but people are coming home from work. A few boaters are out on the lake, and my body is starting to slick with sweat, my pace settling into a rhythm.

My brain is unwinding, beginning to flatten out, and Bryan Adams helps with "(Everything I Do) I Do it For You."

I'm so sorry, Eve. She looked wrecked as we drove home.

I'll build her a new house.

We'll make it through this. I've lived through three timelines to get her back.

I won't lose her again.

I turn onto Cottage Wood, my gait settling into a solid rhythm.

There's something bothering me that I've never really nailed down. Why was Gretchen Anderson killed two years earlier than her previous date of death?

Something spooked Fitzgerald.

I met her in the emergency room, after having gone round with Fitzgerald. According to my memory, they were already dating.

Did she confront him about our fight?

I'm trying not to blame myself for her earlier death, but if I was looking at the case, I'd at least call me an accessory.

I turn onto Minnetonka Boulevard and run downhill, past the school. I can't help but glance toward the ditch where I totaled my beautiful Camaro some twenty-four years earlier and last week.

Saved Danny's life doing it, though. Worth it.

Boston kicks in with, "More Than a Feeling." I crank it and ramp up my speed.

But it's not so loud that I don't hear the car coming up on my tail. An engine revs behind me, and I realize I'm on the wrong side of the road.

I edge closer to the ditch and look over my shoulder.

The car—a Lexus, mind you—is coming at me, dipping over the white line, arrowing toward me.

What the—I leap into the ditch, falling and rolling down the small gully.

The car skims the side of the road, as if it might cartwheel down after me, then rights itself and the driver floors it.

I scramble to my feet and up to the road, hoping for a glimpse at the license plate. *ENJ997.*

Maybe it was an accident, but I don't think so, do you?

I slow to a walk, my heartbeat on high. My body is shaking, and I bend over, holding my knees.

Then I hear the engine again. I look up, and it's turned around. The Lexus is black, a two-door sedan and I squint for a stupid second at the driver before I realize he's coming for me again.

For the love of—I take off again, angling down the ditch and this time the car slides over the side, tearing up the grass.

I'm near the school, and it just takes two steps for me to leap for the chain link fence. I haul myself up and over just as the car bumps through the ditch behind me.

I fall to the other side and the Lexus careens back to the road. Brakes squeal and he nearly front ends an oncoming car. But the other car veers into the ditch and the Lexus jerks onto the road and speeds off.

I'm in the dirt, stunned.

The driver of the other car has stopped. It's a woman and she's driving an orange Kia. She gets out, runs around her car, her hand on the hood, looking for damage.

"I don't think he hit you," I say.

She looks over at me. "Did he try to run you down?"

I brush myself off, working my way to my feet. "I think so."

Her eyes are wide. "Do you want me to call the police?"

I puff out a sarcastic laugh. "I am the police."

She says nothing as I climb over the fence again, staring up the street, my blood hot.

"Are you okay?"

She's looking at my hands, and they're shaking. I jam them into my pockets. "I'm fine."

But I'll admit it has me unnerved. I cut through the school, then take a back street home, running faster than I need to.

I'm still on edge as I walk into the house.

"What happened to you?" Danny rises from a stool at the counter. I look down and see that I'm bleeding—a giant scrape down my calf. Probably from where I went over the fence.

"Someone tried to run me down," I mutter. Bets is in the kitchen too and she grabs a couple paper towels and hands them to me.

"You might need a stitch or two."

I study the cut. "It's just a scrape."

"Someone tried to run you down?" Danny says now. "Did you get plates?"

"ENJ997." I rattle the numbers off to him, and he writes them down.

"I'm on this," he says and disappears into his office next to the kitchen.

"Is Eve upstairs?" I ask Bets.

She nods. "There's a first aid kit in the bathroom."

I try not to leave a bloody trail up the stairs as I climb to the second floor, hit the bathroom, find the first aid kit and band aid the wound. Then I strip off my running clothes and jump in the shower.

I've stopped shaking by the time I get out, the residual adrenaline pooling in my gut. I hope Danny found an ID.

I check out the gunshot wound Gene mentioned in the mirror and find at least two scars I don't remember, one on my shoulder. The other on my thigh.

Maybe I should just be glad this old body still works.

I wrap a towel around my hips and head into the bedroom.

Eve is standing at the window, looking out at the lake.

"Hey," I say, closing the door.

She says nothing.

"Eve?" I walk up to her, reaching out but she turns, and stiff arms me.

Huh?

"I knew it," she says, her voice soft, broken. It's now I see that she's crying.

"Knew what?" I say quietly, because you know how it is. I'm entering a minefield.

"I knew you blamed me for Ashley's death."

And she's got me. Because there's no way I'm getting out of this one. My mouth closes.

Then I glance down, to her hand, and see that she's holding my journal. I look back up at her. "You read that in my journal?"

Her mouth tightens. We stand there a long moment in silence, my brain racing.

What happened in Miami? And what does that have to do with Ashley's death?

"Eve," I say, but she steps back as if I'm a leper. I hold up my hands. "I don't know what to say."

"Say that you meant it when you said it didn't matter."

I blink at her. "I meant it," I say quietly, hoping I did.

She stares at me, a tear falling off her chin. "I just wish I believed you."

Then she tosses my journal on the bed and leaves me there, bloody and cold, standing in my towel.

CHAPTER 10

I am so young. So idealistic. So arrogant.

So full of hope.

I've changed into clean shorts and a T-shirt, and after a very quiet dinner with Eve, who made a good show of acting like she's upset about the house, I escaped to her room.

Just me and the past.

My story reads like it should be accompanied by Thin Lizzy singing "The Boys are Back in Town." Like I said, I really thought I was something.

December 1997.

Burke is out of the hospital, out of rehab—Gene fixed him up good—and back on the job. Shelby is still assigned to me, but she's catching on fast. Got a medal for saving me from Hassan. Fine.

I got a lead on Gretchen Anderson's murder from her roommate, the address of her boyfriend, Leo Fitzgerald.

Booker keeps pestering me about meeting him for breakfast.

Eve has it bad for me. I think I might ask her to marry me.

I stare at the page. Really? Okay, kid, well done. The next date is in early January.

Leo Fitzgerald is in the wind. Visited this address—his mother's place. She's sold it and moved to Florida. No sign of Fitzgerald.
Talked to Danny. He said yes.

I skim the next couple entries, about a couple cases I remember solving.

The next entry isn't until March. And my heart goes cold.

I'm finally out of the hospital. They had Booker's service without me. No leads on the shooter. Burke's case, but we fought about it. He might be right—I'm too close.
But the shooter is in the wind. And I can't help but wonder if it was Leo Fitzgerald and our unfinished business from November. I still don't know why I went after him, but the strange out-of-body memories seem to have vanished.
Eve said no.

Eve said *no?*

But at least he, (me? What do I even call myself?), answered my question about how my travel affects, well, my brain.

The next few months read a little like a bad novel, me waxing poetic about Eve and my lonely life. There's mention of a couple other women, but nothing noteworthy.

Then, in June of 1998,

Eve moved to Miami. I understand, of course, with her father the chief. She says I'm too protective. Yeah, right.

But this is worse.
I can't think.
Danny has offered me an undercover position in Duluth, working narcotics. I'm going to take it.

I went to Duluth? My first undercover gig was in Minneapolis, not a city up north, but as you know, things change. I page through, but the next date isn't for five—*five*—years. What? And it sends a chill through me.

I lived. And Eve heard about it all, I know, because she called me. She was crying, even though I told her I was never in danger, but that was a lie. She misses me.
Yeah, well, she should have never left me.

Rembrandt, ol' pal, you are a certified idiot. I almost can't turn the page, but I do.

Danny says I need to take some time, so, I'm in stupid Miami. It's hot. And Eve doesn't know I'm here, yet. I'm going to surprise her.
Because, you know, I miss her, too.

I check the date. Two months later.
Took you long enough.
The next entry is the next day, however, and the words are in big block writing.

I can't believe she did this.
I don't know why I came down here.
I'm over Eve Mulligan. We're done. Forever and ever, Amen.

I still.

Did what?

A knock, and I look up from where I'm sitting on her bed. The door opens.

It's Eve. "Hi."

I put the journal down. "Hi."

"How's your leg?"

I take a look. The bleeding's stopped. It's not as bad as I thought. "I'm fine."

"Dad says the plate comes from a stolen car. Not a Lexus."

"Figures." Although, I have a few ideas who might have lifted it.

She closes the door. "Reliving old decisions?"

"Eve," I say. "I know what I wrote, but I was young, and stupid and—"

"I know." She comes over to me. "I *know*, Rem. Sometimes, I just can't help blaming myself."

"Why did you…" And I'm not sure what to say, except, "Why did you tell me no when I proposed?"

She looks away. "I ask myself that a lot." She sighs, and I don't think I'm going to like her answer. "You're still overprotective, Rem, but back then—I don't know. I just never thought I'd be able to become someone with Dad—and you—hovering over me."

I stare at her. "Me? I don't hover."

"Are you kidding me? Someone broke into my house and you…you lost it."

That doesn't sound like me, does it?

Except, there's a tiny roil building. "Someone *broke into* your house. Did you expect me to stay calm?"

"I didn't expect you to sleep on my sofa for the next two weeks with your gun. Or stalk me home every night."

Shoot. Sadly, that does sound a little like me.

"Truth is, Rem, after Booker died, after you were shot, you changed. You were…angry. And reckless. And it…it scared me."

I'm trying to see myself in her beautiful hazel-green eyes, see the man I was.

Unfortunately, it's a little too easy.

"I know you were hurting, but I just couldn't stand by and watch. So…"

"So you went to Miami."

"And you went undercover."

I did, didn't I? And probably, for sure, got in over my head. I look away, toward the window, the darkness pressing in, despite the starlight.

"I wanted to see if I could love someone else."

She *what?* I look at her, and she has my gaze in her grip. "You did the same." A long sigh. "It's a small world, Rem. I know you dated other women."

How could she not?

I'm holding the truth is in my hands, and now I hate young, stupid me. I might have been better off not knowing. I have nothing of response but the truth. "My heart was broken." And then, just because I want her to be sure, "There's never been anyone for me but you, Eve."

Her eyes glisten. "Me too."

I don't need to read the rest of the journal. So Eve took up with someone else. The important part is that she came back to me, right?

I touch her face. "I don't know how I got so lucky, really."

She captures my hand, leans against it.

I take a breath. "After Mickey was taken, I spent every night for years—*years*—replaying it in my head. Wishing I'd turned around and gone back for him."

"I know."

"That's the thing, though. I've spent my *entire life* looking back. Wishing I'd done something differently. And…I just keep screwing it up."

She's sitting quietly, just listening.

But there's more, and somehow…she has to know what I know. "Eve, I keep having dreams of Ashley of…well, she's seven years old. And she has this golden blonde hair, and she's swinging on a swing set I made her and…" My eyes are filling. "I wish you could see that dream."

She touches my cheek. "I do, sometimes, Rem. I have the same dream. I really do. Maybe it's real, somewhere."

It is.

"Like heaven."

I nod again. "Probably."

She takes my hand. "I felt the same way after Ashley was born. Wishing I could go back and do something differently. She was so little. I remember her entire hand folded around my fingers. Four pounds, three ounces. I was so scared."

I breathe in deep, imagining it.

"But she lived, and I thought…we're going to be fine, right? After three miscarriages, we finally had our child." Her eyes are full. "I remember her first full out asthma attack. You were so calm. You held her, nebulized her, and I thought…he can do anything."

Asthma. "I'm so sorry I couldn't save her," I say, and I know that sounds crazy, but it feels like the right thing.

"I know you do. But you couldn't have done anything, Rem. By the time you got there, she was gone."

I couldn't have done anything.

"Neither could you. Why do you think I blame you?" I ask softly.

She meets my eyes. "Because I blame myself."

"Eve."

She doesn't look at me.

"I don't want to keep looking back and wishing. It's time to move forward. To grab hold of what I have." I reach over and touch her hand. "You. Me. Us. That's enough."

She meets my eyes and weaves her hands into mine. "Are you sure?"

"Yes." I let out a breath. "Without question."

And I don't know what she thinks she did to cause Ashley's death, but I don't care. "I love you, Eve."

She grabs my shirt and leans in, touching her head to my chest. "Can you forgive me?"

"I will forgive you of anything," I say. "I just wish I'd come after you sooner."

For the first time, I get a smile. "Oh, Val would have loved that."

Val. Her partner, maybe. I'm about to ask, but she kisses me.

And when Eve kisses me, I stop thinking.

She tastes of the summer breeze that's filtering into the window, the night soft around us. When she leans back, she whispers, "Remember when we sneaked into my house to get Asher's help on a case?"

I nod.

"Let's sneak out."

"We're adults, we don't have to—"

But she puts her finger on my lips and we're in some kind of fantasy, apparently. She takes my hand and opens her door.

It's late. I didn't realize how late until now. Her parent's door is closed, and outside, the lake laps the shore in rhythmic, soft hushes.

She tiptoes down the hallway, and into Asher's room.

"Eve—"

"The ladder is still up."

Twenty-four years later? And then I realize. She put it there. My crazy, beautiful, danger-loving wife planned our escape. Her eyes are shining, and I shake my head, despite my smile. She opens the window. Puts her foot out on the roof.

"Eve—"

"Shh." Then she disappears out the window.

For crying out loud, we're way too old for this. But hello, what am I going to do? I climb out after her. She already on the ladder and making her way down.

It's a sacrifice, but I follow her. Someone has to protect her from herself.

The grass is cool and soft on our bare feet as she takes my hand and pulls me toward the lake.

At the dock she runs ahead and it's only as I step out under the glistening reflection of the lake that I realize she's taken off her shirt.

Oh boy.

The rest of her clothing is dropped on the dock and she dives in before I can catch up.

But I do.

I follow the lure of moonlight and find her warm body.

She laughs, and then, in the cool baptismal waters, we let the past go.

CHAPTER 11

The past is like a jilted lover, showing up to boil my rabbit.

Maybe it knows I'm not playing fate's game anymore, that I'm moving on, but it doesn't play fair.

I'm in the CityPerk coffee shop, flashes of memory at first—me, sitting in the car on stakeout in the early morning hours. The light is dim, shadows long across the street.

The smell of roasting coffee reaches out and lures me in.

It's a dream, I know it is, but I can't stop myself from getting out of my car and going inside, past the planter filled with geraniums, past the menu board advertising homemade butterscotch scones, all the way to the counter.

Maybe I'm just hungry.

Inside, the room is cozy—wicker chairs, slipcovered sofas, pipes in the ceiling. A blackboard with specials hangs behind the counter.

I'm standing outside myself, watching, like I would a crime scene, analyzing it. I see myself order coffee. My gaze lands on the thermoses.

One of them contains a bomb.

The barista is blonde, and she hands me, the *other* me, a cup of coffee. Next to her is a biker with long dreadlocks. He's laughing.

Near the door is the lawyer, nursing his cup at the bar along the window.

And another man.

He's wearing track pants and running shoes. Short blonde hair. A tattoo on his arm.

He looks at me and my heartbeat kicks up, thundering.

There's a breath, a heartbeat of recognition inside my dream.

Leo Fitzgerald.

I gasp, and the sound of it—as if I might have been holding my breath—jerks me out of the dream. Light floods my room, cutting through the slatted blinds and across the tumble of sheets and blankets. I drag in another lungful of air, the image still behind my eyes, and maybe it's this second gasp that makes Eve wake up.

She opens her eyes and lifts herself up on one elbow. "Rem?" She has eighties hair, big and crazy, and then I remember she went to bed with it wet.

There are other memories, but they scatter when she puts her hand on my chest. "You're breathing funny."

"I saw him." I weave my fingers through hers on my bare chest. "I saw Leo Fitzgerald at the coffee shop."

Her frown tells me she's trying to place my words. "The CityPerk shop? You remember him from *twenty-four years* ago?"

"I remember him from my dream." Which seemed so real, didn't it?

"He's not in the report," she says and sits up. She's wearing my T-shirt, and I'm trying to remember if we retrieved her clothes from the dock last night.

I know we're married, but I feel suddenly seventeen, afraid of what Eve's father might say. Do we, do I, ever grow out of that?

"He was there, Eve. I'm sure of it. Maybe he left before the police got there, but I saw him."

"You dreamed him." She's trying to tame her hair by pulling it back. "You want this guy, I get that. But I don't understand why you think he's associated with the attempted bombing of CityPerk. He just wasn't there, Rem."

She pulls on a pair of jeans and then heads out of the room, probably for the bathroom.

I get up and find my jeans, too, and then wait in the hall until she's finished. "I know what you're saying, Eve, but it felt a lot more like a *memory* than a dream."

She opens the door, her toothbrush in her mouth. After she spits, she says, "If you want, I'll pull all the interviews of witnesses. Maybe someone saw something from one of the nearby shops." She rinses her mouth and wipes it.

I lean in to kiss her, but she dodges me and moves aside to let me in, and heads to the bedroom to change.

We need our own place, yesterday.

Ten minutes later, I'm out of the shower, my hair wet. I change into dress pants and an oxford, grab my suit coat, then go downstairs and pull up a stool in the kitchen. I don't look out at the dock, although the sun is turning the water a deep platinum.

Eve's made coffee, her auburn hair pulled back in a tight bun, and she's wearing a pair of dress pants and a blouse. I think she must have raided her mom's closet.

Danny is up too, and drinking a cup of coffee, reading the morning paper. He's old school—believes in paper journalism rather than getting his news from morning TV.

Eve pours me a mug full as Danny closes the paper.

"What were you thinking?"

I look over at him (Eve does too) and he slides the paper down to me.

The front-page headline is brutal. *Serial Killer Haunting City.*

Great. Mayor Vega is going to have my head.

The article reads close to the information I gave Frankie, although she hints that the killer has stalked the city for two decades.

Zeke has been talking, maybe. She did say he knew about the case.

"You're going to have copycats," Danny says. "And you just scared the stuffing out of every woman in Minneapolis."

"Good," Eve says, rising to my defense. "Women should be afraid. And careful. Armed, even."

Her father looks at her. She raises an eyebrow.

Danny purses his lips.

Well, I wouldn't argue with her either.

"Eggs?" she says and turns to the stove.

I say nothing as she murders a dozen eggs, whipping them into a froth and pouring them into a sizzling pan.

"Did Shelby okay this?" Danny says as the eggs crackle.

"I'm the chief."

"For now."

"I don't want more women dying on my watch." I turn in my chair. "It should have happened sooner."

Danny's mouth tightens. "You mean on *my* watch."

"That's not what I said." And of course, not what I mean. I know who's to blame here.

"Here are your eggs," Eve says, putting a plate down in front of me. It includes bacon.

She gives her father the same. Then leans against the counter, eating a piece of bacon. "Did you unearth anything about the killer from your journal? Anything we missed?"

I should've been a little more direct about what he-slash-me should keep track of. "I have notes about Burke and me tracking down his address, but just that the place belonged to his mother, and that she'd already moved to Florida."

She's studying at me. "Florida? Maybe we should—"

My cell phone vibrates on the counter and I snag it. "Chief Stone."

"Don't let that go to your head," Burke says into my right ear.

"I thought you were on paternity leave."

"It's over. We have a survivor."

For a moment, I haven't a clue what he means. "A survivor."

"Looks like your announcement might have worked. It hit the ten o'clock news last night, and not long after, a woman was leaving her shift at an all-night diner; got attacked."

"But she survived."

"She was roughed up, but yes, she's alive. Used pepper spray. The St. Paul police got the case, but after they interviewed her, they called me."

"Why?"

"Because the perp had a tattoo. And he'd been at the diner earlier that night and handed her a twenty-dollar bill."

I slide off the bench my blood raging. "Was it marked?"

"Yes."

"Did she see her attacker?" I head to the door to grab my shoes. Eve is on my tail, her satchel over her shoulder. "Did she get a description?"

"She did."

Grabbing Danny's keys to his truck, I head outside. "What's her name?"

"Just a sec."

I glance at Eve as I toss her the keys. "We have a witness. A survivor. Because of the article."

"You're a genius," she says.

Hopefully it's enough to keep Vega from tar and feathering me.

I slide into the passenger seat.

We're pulling out of the driveway when Burke comes back on the line. "Her name is Meggie. Meggie Fox. She's in her mid-twenties, and lives—"

In Stillwater.

"—in Stillwater."

I can't breathe.

"Rem?" Eve glances at me, concerned. "You okay?"

I nod.

But you know I'm not okay. Because I know Meggie Fox.

She's the daughter of Arthur Fox, my watch repairman.

She's the one who helped me understand my time travel rewrites.

And in the last go 'round, she died. In the annuals of my memories, I can still hear her father's anguished words. "*You could go back. You could stop him.*"

I feel a little like weeping.

Because, in a way, I did.

"Tell her to stay put. I want to talk to her."

"You got it, Chief."

You think I'd be used to the curve balls by now. But they're not curve balls. They're boomerangs, that keep circling around behind me and smacking in the back of the head.

I look out the window as Eve drives. You might not remember him, but Arthur Fox is a friend, of sorts. I met him two weeks, and decades ago, when John Booker's watch landed in my possession.

When this insane time-travel business began.

Poor Art. I remember Meggie and her lemonade. It's funny

how time knits us all together. And, I probably owe Art an apology because I can't help but believe I somehow got him tangled in this mess, even if this time, Meggie is alive.

"You're scaring me, Rem," Eve says into my thoughts. "You know this girl?"

"I know her father. He used to, um, consult for me."

"Are you sure it's the Jackson killer?"

I nod. Because the past isn't letting go that easily.

We pull into St. Joseph's Hospital, off 10th Street in downtown St. Paul. It's a sleek mirror and wood building that overlooks the capital building, in the heart of downtown. We park and head into the building, to the main floor receptionist. I show my badge and ask for Meggie Fox's room.

I find her on the third floor, at the end of the hall.

A uniform stands guard outside her room. I show my badge again, and then knock on the door.

Burke opens it, and I enter, bracing myself.

It's bad, but she's alive. Sleeping, maybe, because her eyes are closed. Meggie is in her mid-twenties, with shorter blonde hair than I remember, although it's covered in a bandage. She's pretty, but that's from memory because her face is bruised and swollen, a cut on her right cheek is stitched but left unbandaged.

Her arm is in a sling, her wrist cast, and she has ligature marks around her neck.

I've seen plenty of crime scenes, of course, but seeing Meggie like this—I don't know why but my gorge wants to rise. Maybe it's the fact that this is final, this timeline is the one that will take.

She'll forever have this terrible memory, and I can't change it.

"She's been sleeping for about an hour," Burke says quietly. "But I wanted to stick around until you got here."

"Inspector Stone?" The voice comes from a man standing at

the window. I recognize him—this version of Art is the one I remember from our last meeting. He's in his mid-sixties, and has dark, graying hair. He's always struck me a little like an earnest yet wild-eyed professor. His brown eyed gaze widens as he holds out his hand. "I remember you."

I walk over and shake his hand. "It's a been while." Four days, at least. Okay, I'm just being funny, but we time travelers have to at least try to have a sense of humor. *Former* time travelers.

He looks at Eve and Burke, conversing near the door, then back to me, and leans close. "How is the watch working?"

Full disclosure, I've met Art a number of times. The first time, I brought him my broken watch and he shut the door on my face and told me it was working just fine, thank you. Which, as it turns out, it was. Then I visited him in the past, with the same question and I blurted out the truth.

It's this memory he has of me now, probably, although we also met when I saved him from a deadly car accident.

So, just to divert any crazy questions he might pose, I say, "How's your wife?"

Sheila.

"She's distressed. Down at the chapel, I believe. But—" He looks at Meggie. "It could have been much worse."

My mouth tightens and his eyes widen. His voice lowers. "Was it much worse?"

I know what he's referring to. He knows I travel. That I change things.

That those things touch him. So, I give him a small, imperceptible nod.

He's released my hand, but now glances at my wrist. I have a crazy urge to cover up my naked wrist, as if embarrassed. Frowning, he meets my eyes.

"I don't have it," I say before he can ask. "It's lost."

He opens his mouth, maybe to ask how in the world could I lose something like the watch when Meggie moans, coming around. Art moves to her bedside. "Megs?"

She rouses, wincing.

I hate that this has happened to her, but I need answers.

I wait until her she looks up at me. "Meggie, are you up to answering some questions?"

She nods. I remember her as spunky, and some of that flashes in her eyes now.

"My partner Burke," I start, before I realize my faux pas. But it's a habitual statement, so I continue. "Interviewed you. Said you saw your attacker. Can you describe him again for me? Maybe run me through the attack again?"

As I stand there, I see another woman, bruising around her neck, her eye blackened, her soft voice telling me about how her attacker chased her, put his foot into her back to hold her down. How he kept apologizing even as he assaulted her.

Hollie Larue. Her murder case now sits on my desk.

But Meggie is alive, and that's another tick on my side of the scoreboard. If we're keeping score.

Which you know I am.

"I don't remember much about the attack." Her voice is soft, but surprisingly strong. "Just that I'd seen the news that night, and so I waited inside the diner for my Uber."

"You called an Uber?"

"My car wouldn't start—"

"I should have junked that thing," Art says. "I should have bought you a new one."

"Dad—I can take care of myself."

"He'll get you a new one," I say as I glance at Art who gives a quick nod. "Go on."

"I saw a car drive up, and I thought maybe it was the Uber, so I went outside. But…" She swallows, closes her eyes. "When I got closer, I realized it wasn't so I turned to go back inside…and that's when he got out."

"He got out of the car?"

"Yeah. So, I took off for the building, but he was fast. He caught up by the time I reached the door and slammed his hand on it and grabbed me."

Art is looking away.

"Art, do you need to step—" Eve starts.

"No."

I don't blame him. But Meggie might talk more freely without him. "Art. Maybe it's easier for Meggie if you wait outside."

He looks at me like he'd like to turn me to cinder. But his mouth tightens, and he leans over Meggie. "I'll be right outside."

"I'll be okay."

He doesn't acknowledge her, and I see the doubt on his face as he walks past me.

I understand that look.

I've worn that look.

"Then what happened, Meggie," Eve says, when the door closes.

"I elbowed him, and broke away from him, and just started running. I know it sounds stupid, but I couldn't think, I just…I just ran."

"Did he chase you?"

"Yes. It was dark, and late, and maybe I thought I could lose him, but he was faster. He jumped on me and got me on the ground. I was kicking, and screaming, and somehow, I'd gotten a hold of the pepper spray in my bag." She looks at me. "I saw the

116

news, right before I left, and I normally keep it in my car, but I thought…maybe…"

I glance at Eve.

"He hit me, and I nearly blacked out, then he put his hands around my throat—And that's when I pepper-sprayed him."

She stops for a breath, and I can see she's fighting back tears. Then a quick swallow and she continues. "He sort of shouted, and rolled off me, and that's when I got up and kept running. Only this time I went back to the diner. Unfortunately, I tripped on a parking curb, but I landed right in the parking lot, in front of a couple college students."

"Is that when you broke your wrist," Eve says.

She nods.

"That's a nasty cut," I say. "How did you get it?"

"When he hit me. I think he wore a ring. I remember the cold on my throat—I know, that sounds strange, but it keeps coming to me. It's like, as I struggled, my brain started to disconnect, to dissect everything. The smell of him—"

"You remember how he smelled?"

"Yeah. It was…like soiled, you know? Like old gym clothes."

I remember Hollie Larue saying the same thing. Details, it's always the little details.

"Meggie, do you remember him talking? Saying anything?" Like, apologizing as he was hurting her? I want to ask, but I don't want to skew her testimony. Still, I'm hoping—

She looks at me, and slowly nods. "Yeah, actually. After he hit me, he cursed, as if he was angry that he'd done it. And when he put his hands around my neck, he was sort of, almost whimpering. Like it hurt him, too. And he kept saying, 'I'm sorry. I'm sorry.' And that I should be quiet."

Eve is looking at me but I don't surrender to her gaze.

117

Because I got that from Hollie, too, in a timeline Eve will never know.

"Do you remember what his ring looked like?"

She shakes her head. "But I do remember what he looks like. He's tall. And muscular. He was wearing a baseball cap at the diner, but I think he has blonde hair. I remember waiting on him, although, I don't remember the smell. Or the ring. He did leave me a tip, though. A twenty-dollar bill."

Burke is nodding, his mouth a grim line.

"It had words on it—Thank you for your service."

The one detail we left out of the news article.

I glance at Eve. "Do you think we could get a sketch artist in here?"

She nods.

"Thank you, Meggie," I say, and motion for Burke to join me outside.

He follows me, as does Eve. I look at them. "We've thought he was an athlete for a while, but maybe that's why he chases them. He likes the competition. But, why the apology?"

"Maybe he was raised with a militant sense of right and wrong," Burke says.

"Conservative? Religious?"

"Could be why he tips them," Eve says.

"He was also in the military," Burke adds, a tidbit he probably doesn't like, given his service record.

"Yeah, but before or after he started killing?" I'm thinking of the bodies in my backyard. I turn to Eve. "I need shots of that crime scene, but especially her wound. I'd like to know what kind of ring might leave that type of mark."

Eve pulls out her phone and walks away from us.

I turn to Burke. "The smell. I know that smell. Makes me

think of Quincy's. And the way my gear smells after a week of sweating in it."

"You think this guy wears his old gym clothes when he's hunting?"

"Could be part of his ritual. Signify something he's trying to recreate, maybe. Let's get a hold of all the boxing gyms in the area and run the tattoo and the sketch we get through their database, see if we get any hits."

Burke nods. "Good call on the article."

"We'll see if Vega agrees."

"Shelby will be so jealous." He winks.

"I'll bet." I see Art leaning against the wall, his back to me and walk over to him. "Hey, Art."

He swallows and runs his finger and thumb across his eyes before he turns.

"How you doing?"

He shakes his head. But draws in a breath, and again glances at my wrist. "How'd you lose it?"

"Time glitch. The guy who gave it to me—"

"Chief Booker."

Wow, he has a good memory. "Yeah. He died before he could hand it over to me."

"So, it's gone."

I lift a shoulder. "I don't know. It could be buried with him."

He looks down the hall, past me, then back. "You changed this. Something."

I nod.

"She was dead before."

Again.

"I should be grateful."

I lift a shoulder. "I don't know. I can't help but feel like somehow, by my going to you in the first place—"

"No." He shakes his head. "Everything you do, or did, has ramifications. A butterfly flaps its wings in the Amazon, and a storm ravages half of Europe. Edward Lorenz, the butterfly effect. You can't predict—or be blamed for what happened."

His words should give me relief, but I'm staring at the ravages of my choices in his broken face, so I've got nothing. But I have questions, and he's the only one who might have answers. So, "Art, I have a problem. I'm recalling things I don't remember. Memories I shouldn't have. It's like my brain is divided."

He nods. "Remember what I said about your consciousness traveling outside time when you chronothize? Your brain is starting to sync with the memories you've created in this overwrite. Eventually, these new memories will take over."

His words have me by the throat. "I could forget my daughter?"

"The daughter you left behind in your first timeline."

The only daughter I remember.

I refuse to forget Ashley, even if I'm the only one. But without the watch, my only hope is to fix what I started, and live with what remains. I push the weight of that from mind. For now.

"I have another problem. My boss—John Booker—changed something. He went back in my timeline and found my brother's murderer…and everyone else remembers a different history. But shouldn't I remember this, too?"

"Yes. And you will, in time."

I can't seem to get it out of my head … this image of Booker sitting in my-slash-his office, telling me about the one absolute; to not mess with time. I ignored him.

Art looks me in the eye. "Don't beat yourself up, Inspector. Just…find this guy. Stop him. And pray you don't need that watch ever again."

Then he says the words that send the chill down my spine. "Stay Stalwart, Inspector."

Stalwart. The word on the back of Booker's watch. I swallow, but nod.

We both might need those words more than ever. He heads back to Meggie's room as Eve returns.

"Remember what you said about Florida?" She wears a smile that looks like trouble.

Uh oh. I haven't a clue, but I nod anyway.

"Maybe we need to pay a visit to Leo Fitzgerald's mother."

Right. That. "Do you know where she is?"

She smiles. "I have friends in Florida, remember?"

Not even a little. But I'm in. "Book us flights."

Besides, I'm ready to find out what happened in Florida, aren't you?

CHAPTER 12

There's a tight band around my chest I'm trying to ignore as Eve and I board our flight to Miami.

Truth is, Art's words are looping through my mind, like a song, over and over, and it has me in a knot. *Pray you don't need that watch ever again.*

I'm not going to panic. But he's right.

As soon as I started to time travel, life was no longer fixed in place.

Outcomes could be changed.

Lives repaired, and a better—happier—ending at my fingertips.

In theory.

Now, I have to live with what I get, just like the everyone else.

Eve and I are traveling light. Her contacts in Miami (and no, I'm not asking too many questions, yet), dug up Helen Fitzgerald's address at a residential care facility outside the city. I called to confirm, but I didn't talk to her.

I don't want to spook her.

We're close, I can feel it in my bones.

I have no recollection of ever being in Miami. We took a trip to Hawaii for our fifth anniversary, so I've seen the ocean before, but as we angle over the city, I'm caught by the massive expanse of water along the shore, so much blue, extending to the horizon.

Having grown up near a lake, I'm not afraid of the water. But there's a part of me that is mesmerized by what lies beneath. I suppose it's that same part of me that decided traveling back in time might be a good idea. What did Eve call it—reckless?

Maybe. But that was then.

Now, I'm smarter, right? (Don't answer that, thanks).

I do feel about twenty-eight when I discover Eve has rented a Corvette convertible for our quick tour through Miami. I put the top down in the parking garage while she pulls up her GPS to the Cyprus Gardens Senior Care Center.

She looks over at me. "Miss that Camaro, don't you?"

"And my Porsche."

"Right. You were born for speed."

I don't know why, but I have urge to flex as I pull out of the garage, my sunglasses on, the hot wind in my hair. The air is heavy, filled with the lure of palm trees and beach even as I move toward the highway.

Like me, Eve is wearing her office clothes, but I notice she's pulled off her shoes, leaving her feet bare. Her hair is wild and free, and she leans back and closes her eyes.

I wonder just how much she loved Miami.

Her phone rings just as I hit the on ramp to I-95.

"Stay on this for twenty-four miles." She answers the phone. "Director Stone here."

I miss the manual transmission as I dart in and out of traffic. Eve covers one ear as she talks. I hear her mention the tattoo we sent out statewide. Then, "Yes. We'll be right there."

She looks at me and motions toward the next exit. I get over as she hangs up. "That was Val," she says, like I know exactly who she's talking about. "The tattoo turned up a hit. A guy matching Fitzgerald's description works for a trucking company based out of the harbor. All their employees have to have a background check, and their file is kept in our—rather, the Miami Police Department database."

"Seriously?" I take the exit but pull over at the first gas station.

"Yeah," she says, the sky glinting off her sunglasses, bright and sunny. "And what's better, he's supposed to be coming in from a run tonight."

Tonight. I do the math— "Wait. Are you saying he's on the road?"

"I don't know."

The math doesn't work, does it? Because Fitzgerald is supposed to be in Minnesota, cooling off after his crime.

More, if Meggie slathered him with pepper spray, odds are he wouldn't be driving anytime soon.

Still, it's worth a look. "Where to?"

"Val says to meet him at his office."

Him.

Now, you thought Val was a woman, didn't you? Me too.

"Super," I say.

She pulls up the directions and we navigate to the police station while my brain conjures up all sorts of Val-related questions.

Was Val her partner?

Was Val the one she tried falling for?

Was Val the reason she came home? (And the answer to that is no. She came home for me, remember?)

I know these aren't the answers we came for, but I can't help it.

I'm an investigator, and Eve is suddenly a mystery to me.

The Miami Police Department headquarters is located downtown in a massive concrete and glass structure surrounded by palm trees. We park in a nearby lot and I follow Eve into the lobby. It's all black tile and sleek lines and I can't help but compare it to the stately and ornate Romanesque fortress that is our City Hall.

But maybe that's the way they are down here. Flashy and slick. With guys named Val and Sonny and Rico. With fast cars and sleek boats and tans—

I feel a little overdressed in my suit as I hang back and wait for Eve's...friend.

Admittedly, I'm expecting white parachute pants, a collarless shirt and Ray-Bans, but Val shows up out of the elevator wearing suit pants and a white shirt, rolled up past his elbows, a stark contrast to his dark skin. He's handsome, wears his hair short to his scalp, and is bigger than me. Not that that bothers me. Really.

He possesses a sort of confidence about him that's supposed to tell me he has nothing to prove. But he's not wearing a ring and he's just a little too friendly with 'his girl Eve, whatdoyaknow' who he pulls into a tight hug and kisses on her cheek.

Okayyyyy.

"And this must be Rembrandt," he holds out his hand, still friendly and maybe it's me who has something to prove. "Detective Valentine Castillo."

I meet his eyes. *She's my girl, not yours,* I say with mine.

He smiles, nods and the game is on.

Listen, I know how it sounds, but that's just the way it is. Eve is the prize, and although I've won, I have a feeling there are coups yet uncounted.

"Listen, I found your guy, and I talked with the dispatcher. He's due to come in tonight around eight. He had a short haul from Atlanta today."

"Did he start in Atlanta?" Because I'm still doing math.

"I don't know," he says. "It's only about ten hours on the turn-pike."

So he could have gotten on a flight, landed in Atlanta and ended up tonight in Miami.

Where we wouldn't think to look for him.

For twenty-four years?

I check my watch. It's nearly six p.m.

"I figure we'll head over there in an hour or so, stake it out, and see if we can catch him." He looks at Eve. "Hungry?"

"Chef Creole?"

"I know you love your conch fritters."

"And fresh slaw?"

She says it slow, the syllables drawn out, the ending more of an "ow," and I can't contain a look of horror because she just winks at me.

What is going on?

Val swings his keys around his finger as we head back out into the sun. It's low, its long dusky fingers threading through the buildings. I'd like to take the Corvette, but apparently, we're taking his car.

Appropriately, a Dodge Charger. Yeah, well, I've got two more cylinders and 650 horses under the hood of my, um, rental.

He opens Eve's door and pushes back the seat of his two-door. Waits.

I climb inside.

"Rem—I'll sit in back—" Eve starts but I just hold up my hand.

I'll sit back here. Someone just turn up the air conditioning. I'm already sweltering.

Val wears a gold bracelet on his wrist. As he pulls out into the city, he turns off the hip hop on his radio. "Eve and I used to hit up this place for lunch." He glances over at Eve. "An alternative to donuts, right?"

She laughs, almost a giggle.

What is *happening*?

"You know, the thing about conch—like most seafood—is it's an aphrodisiac. And usually it makes you get, um, a little more personal, right? But we use it to focus on solving our cases."

Sure you do. I lean back and fold my arms, watching, my teeth grinding a little. Val's so friendly with other people's wives, he should have a dentist on retainer.

Miami is a well used town, the buildings showing wear, graffiti on the underpasses. I'm sure it has better areas, but I can't see much out of the tiny triangle windows.

My shirt is soaked through by the time we pull up to a little open air diner, grease so thick in the air I feel it land on my skin like salt. Pictures of conch and other seafood specialties hang above the counter like specials at a coffee shop. Patrons sit at the counter, eating out of foam containers.

Val orders for us without asking—I let it go—and Eve takes me over to a row of counter stools affixed to the pavement, facing out to the street.

Whatever.

"Seems like he knows you pretty well," I say.

She's sipping on a lemonade she got from a giant bubbler in front. "We worked together. He trusted me."

My mouth tightens, and she laughs. "Rem. Calm down. Val is nice. And a great detective."

At the moment I don't care what kind of detective he is. Because what I wanted to hear was the standard "we just worked together," defense.

I didn't hear that, did you?

I try not to, but my gaze drifts back over to Val. He's built, wide shoulders, and he's laughing with the gals behind the counter. He sort of reminds me of Burke, a solid presence about him.

Someone emerges from the kitchen with three containers and he carries them over to the bar and hands us each one. I open it up and the smell of cayenne pepper and garlic strips the skin off my nose. The conch is fried to a deep golden brown, and layered with lime slices, green peppers and dipping sauce.

"Your eyes are going to roll back into your head," Eve says and picks up one of the fritters, then dips it into the sauce.

As if fate is trying to intervene, an old Chevy Impala drives by, sits at the light, blasts out Boston's, "Peace of Mind."

"So, what's the story on this Fitzgerald guy?" Val asks as he dips his conch, leaning over his tray so he doesn't drip on his fancy, no-sweat-at-all white shirt.

"He's a serial killer," I say, picking up my conch. "Been on the run for twenty some years." I stare at my conch. "What is this?"

"Seafood," Eve says. She's on her third fritter and isn't shy about the dip. "You know those big shells that you can hear the ocean in?"

"You can't really hear the ocean," Val the tour guide says.

"Yeah, I know but…."

She doesn't finish, and I'm refraining from adding, *but this idiot doesn't.*

I know. Stop, Rem.

"It's good," I say, and hate myself a little for admitting that. But I'm making nice for Eve.

Val looks over at me, grinning. The smile seems genuine. Maybe he's not a total jerk. Maybe.

"Eve and I sometimes picked up conch before we headed out

to Miami Beach, right?"

Okay, that's enough.

Eve grins. "They had the best bands—we saw Journey there once."

I look at her. Really?

"Val introduced me to all sorts of new music."

Did he now? I try another conch, but I've lost my appetite. I wipe my hands and sit back. "Leo Fitzgerald first started killing in 1997 although we recently found five more victims that predate that." I don't mention that it was in my—

"They were in Rem's backyard," Eve says. "So, clearly, the killer is playing a game with him."

"Wow." Val frowns. "Any idea why?"

"I don't—" I start, but Eve interrupts me.

"Rem tracked him down in his early days, and tried to arrest him, but he got away."

When did Eve turn into Miss Chatty?

"Whew, that's rough," Val says. "Twenty plus years playing his game. That's gotta hurt." Val finishes off his last conch. "Good thing he's in our backyard, now. We'll get him." He's wiping off his hands.

I lean forward. "He strangles them. Chases them down after their shift—most of them are waitresses, or bartenders, although a few have been hookers—and after he's done, he leaves a tip. A twenty-dollar bill." I give Eve a look and her eyes widen. Because I'm fishing, but I don't want to give anything away. "Have you had any crimes that fit that MO?"

The thing is, if he says yes, then this case slips like sand through my fingers and becomes the property of the FBI.

Leo is my fault. He's my collar.

Val shakes his head. "We've had a number of waitresses and

bartenders killed on my watch, but...no, nothing like that." He takes Eve's empty tray and stacks it with his own. "Our last serial killer was Sam Little. Guy killed ninety women over the span of thirty years. Most of them here. So, I get ya."

I'm not sure he does, but I nod anyway.

"You gonna finish that?"

"Nope." I throw my napkin on top of the basket. "I don't need an aphrodisiac to help me catch this guy," I say, no smile.

Eve raises an eyebrow. The sun is low, hot and lethal on the horizon and I'm ready to go.

Val follows me out to his car, and bleeps the door unlocked. I climb in the back, ignoring Eve's protests.

Val slides into the front seat. "I love a good stakeout." He looks at Eve and winks.

She laughs.

Oh, this is going to be fun.

CHAPTER 13

I'm having a blast. Best stakeout ever.

The air is a washcloth on my skin as it filters in through the open window of the Charger.

Although, admittedly not *much* air, here in the back seat. My shirt is soggy and we're sitting near the entrance to the container yard of Seaboard Shipping, the outfit that employs Leo Fitzgerald.

The guy is employed as Lee Fitzgerald, but the photo ID Eve pulled from his military records matches the record on file with the shipping company, and his recent check in with dispatch said he's on his way.

It's just a waiting game.

So here we sit. I'm in a knot in the ever-so-expansive back seat of the charger, listening to Val and Eve continue to talk old times. And continue.

Homicides they investigated together. Gang killings in Little Havana. A mother shot in the elite area of Coconut Grove. A serial killer in the Pork and Beans district, wherever that is. They mention halfway houses, and strip clubs, college students missing on the beach, and the time they evacuated angry residents before one of the many hurricanes hit the area.

So. Much. Fun.

I feel like the proverbial third wheel on a date Val is having. With. My. Wife.

Every once in a while, Val looks back at me and grins, clearly happy having me captive in the back seat. Eve can't see me in the darkness, as I'm sitting right behind her.

Probably a good thing.

Seaboard Shipping has an entrance off the main road for their office, and another for receiving, where the big trucks come in. Val has us parked across the lot from the office, but the big crane to off-load the trucks into the container yard is some hundred feet away.

If he pulls up there, first, and sees us waiting, he might get spooked. And I'm jammed into to the backseat.

The odors of the shipyard—oil and grease, the brine of the sea, the scent of gasoline—filter in, adding to the souring fried conch in my gut.

Maybe Val was right about the aphrodisiac helping him focus.

I'm very, *very* focused. Mostly about wrapping my hands around Val's neck and squeezing hard, but I'm pretty sure that's not what he meant.

Mariana Vega has called three times, by the way. Left two voicemails, which I haven't listened to. My hope is she'll stop ha-rassing me when I bring back the Jackson killer.

But sitting in the back, trying to ignore their stories has given me time to think. And I think I've figured out Leo's MO; why we haven't found him.

He's been driving for Seaside Shipping for nearly fifteen years. Which makes sense—the killings slowed down for a gap of five years after Gretchen Anderson died. He probably fled, then found his way back to Minnesota while hauling freight across the country.

Stopped in at diners, or bars, found his quick victim, and left the state the next morning.

Sneaky.

Not anymore.

The night has settled around us, just a floodlight over the door of the building. "I'm getting out," I say, interrupting a riveting memory of a celebrity chef murdered in one of the elite restaurants on the strip. "I need a better vantage point."

Eve stops talking and turns around. "Really? What if he sees you?"

"He won't see me. Please let me out." I'm trying not to be short with her. After all, I'm sure Burke and I can bore her to death when we hash out old crimes. Still, maybe she senses my irritation because she gets out. Val puts his hand over the dome light, and I make it quick, pushing the seat forward and practically falling out of the back seat.

I can't feel my feet.

"You stay inside, though," I say to Eve, touching her arm. "This guy is dangerous, and I don't want you anywhere near him."

The words remind me, suddenly, of the day she went to Midtown Ink in Minneapolis, hunting down Fitzgerald's address from a tattoo artist. It so freaked me out—the idea of her getting close to Leo—that I pulled her into an alleyway and begged her not to get involved.

But mostly, I remember kissing her.

That was the day I decided I would never let anything happen to Eve. So maybe I was a bit overprotective, but can you blame me?

Fitzgerald is dangerous.

I meet her eyes now, in the dim glow of the dome light. "Please," I add.

She nods, her mouth a tight line. Then, suddenly, she grabs

135

my soggy shirt, leans over and kisses me.

It shocks me so much I barely have time to lean into it.

It's not a long kiss, but definitely purposeful, and I wonder if she knows I've been sitting in the back seat, stewing, (and not just metaphorically.) Probably does. After all, it is Eve.

The driver's side door also opens, now, and Val gets out. "I think you're right. Let's go mobile and move closer to the entrance."

"Eve is staying here," I say, just to remind him who is in charge.

He nods, and Eve gets back in the car. "Call for backup if you think we need it."

She closes her door and the night goes dark again.

Val walks over to a nearby container, across the road from the entrance, and slips into the shadows. I follow him and lean against the wall of the container. The heat soaks through my shirt and I step away.

"Yeah, these things are frying pans after they've been cooking all day in the sun," Val says. Except for his white shirt he'd be invisible in the darkness.

Silence falls between us.

Then, "I have to admit, Stone. You're being a good sport about all of this. I half expected a repeat of our last meeting."

I fold my arms, not looking at him, because I might not remember, but I can probably guess what happened. "That was a long time ago."

"True. And I guess you won, in the end."

Won the fight? Or won the girl? Probably both. I say nothing.

"Does Eve ever talk about it?"

I look at him. "Talk about what?"

He's quiet, then, "The baby."

The—the *what?*

I say nothing as I try to mentally scramble to my feet.

"It wasn't her fault, you know. She didn't realize she was pregnant—neither of us did. Not until it was too late."

I can't breathe, the night suddenly suffocating.

"I just wanted you to know that I really loved her. And I would have married her if—well, if she wasn't so hooked on you."

I glance at him, then.

"We tried, or I tried, after you left, to piece us back together, but…maybe we were always destined to be just friends."

And I was destined to be her husband. I guess I can thank fate for that.

"I'll be honest though, I was worried about her."

I'm frowning now, and maybe he can see me, because, "You were every bit the hothead she'd described you as."

"I'm not—"

"I'll never forget that day her dad called. Told us about how you'd nearly died in some undercover gig near the border. She completely freaked out." He pauses. "That's when I knew it was over between us. You coming down here and making a scene just delayed the inevitable. But you should probably know, I didn't like it." His tone hardens. "Truth is, Stone, I'm still not sure you deserve Eve. Not sure you're not going to do something stupid and get killed and break her heart."

His words sink into me as I try to process the new information. The silence between us stretches out to an uncomfortable length so I finally speak. "You're probably right," I say to him quietly. "I don't deserve Eve. But, I do love her. And I'd give my life for her."

"I'm sure you would. But would you save your life—for her? Step away from danger, let it go if you had to?"

Lights cutting into the shipyard silence my answer. If I had one that is, because I don't know. Yes? Of course?

Because I did that, once upon a time. Walked away from the

job, left it all behind.

But my regrets pulled me back in, and that says something.

I'm a cop, right to my bones, like Eve said, and maybe it's time I acknowledge that.

I step back, away from the scrape of headlights, and watch as a truck pulls in. It's a semi, with a container on the bed, and the driver leaves it running as he climbs out.

The semi coughs, and I look at Val, motion with my head. "I need a closer look."

Val nods, I think, and I take off for the building.

Leo has gone inside.

I don't want a struggle inside the office. Leo is dangerous, and someone might get hurt. So, I wait outside, ready to ambush him. And I mean *catch him off guard*, not hurt him, just to be clear. Because I *have* changed, Val, thank you very much.

Leo Fitzgerald is a big man. He easily stands six feet three or four, a good two-sixty on his muscular frame, and he's wearing a baseball cap, just like Meggie said. That, and jeans and a pullover.

The dispatcher is talking with him. Leo signs papers, then probably gets told where to park his truck.

I ease back, out of the light as he heads to the door.

It opens, and I take a breath.

He's out into the parking lot, before I step out. "Leo Fitzgerald—"

I don't get halfway before Val is standing in front of the guy. "Stop right there. Fitzgerald, you're under arrest for suspicion of murder."

Thanks, Val. And right after we had a moment.

Leo doesn't stop his gait, doesn't hesitate, just advances on Val, two quick steps, and smacks the gun away with one hand. He puts a fist in Val's face with the other.

Val falls like an anvil. The gun goes spinning into the darkness.

"Fitzgerald," I say, stepping out of the darkness. I've pulled my gun, of course. "Stop!"

He acts like he doesn't hear me because he scoops up Val's gun. Turns. And then he fires at me.

What the—?

I dive behind the truck, breathing hard. His feet pound against the pavement as he heads toward the entrance.

Toward Eve.

I scramble out from behind the truck, my brain set on panic.

And then I spot Eve. She's gotten out of the car, her own weapon pulled. Leo is running toward the gate.

"Stop!" she shouts.

My life stops as Fitzgerald points his gun at her and shoots.

"Eve!"

She's down, and I'm not sure if she's hurt, but my voice has turned Fitzgerald on me. He shoots once, again, a third time, as I duck and move and scramble toward Eve.

Oh God, no—

He veers away from the gate, and Eve, and heads down into the container yard. Shoots again.

I dive behind a parked car, still twenty feet away from her. "Eve!"

I'm a freakin' puddle of relief when she shouts, "I'm okay!"

Yeah, well, I won't believe her until I see her. Fitzgerald is still running, but he's stopped shooting, so I find my feet and run.

Eve is crouched on the far side of the Charger, holding her weapon, when I slide into her position. I holster my weapon and grab her shoulders. "Are you hit? Are you okay?"

"I'm fine!" She jabs a finger in the direction of Leo. "But he's getting away!"

I stand up, trying to find him, and spot a figure in the distance—wow, he can run—in the far end of the yard.

"Stay here—!" I pull my gun again and take off.

He might be fast, and I might not have my twenty-eight-year-old body, but I'm still in decent shape.

And I had a conch fritter or two. I have adrenaline.

I get about twenty feet from Leo when I hear her voice, a dim shout behind me. "Rem! Val's been shot!"

Stifling a word, I slow, watching Leo disappearing into the night and okay, I'll admit I considered just…

Give me a break. I've been looking for Leo for more than twenty years. Or two weeks. But it feels like over two decades.

But I'm not that guy, and Val's in my head with his challenge as I turn and sprint back to them. *But would you save your life—for her? Step away from danger, let it go if you had to?*

She's on the ground, her hand to his chest. Val is writhing, clearly still alive, wracked with pain. "Call 911!" she shrieks.

The dispatcher has come out, too, and is on the phone. "Help is on the way!"

"Hang in there, Val," I say as I take off my shirt, then wad it up and use it to stanch the bleeding. "I got this, Eve." She leans away, shaking as I press on his wound. "Stay with us, Val. We got ya."

He wraps his hand around my wrist, and his eyes meet mine. "Sorry."

"It's okay. We'll get him next time." I say that without a burr in my throat.

Instead, the burr is in my chest as Val's grip slips away, and his eyes close. "Val—c'mon buddy…"

And beside me, Eve is weeping.

CHAPTER 14

There's so much. So much, I don't know where to start.

First—Val is still alive and in surgery by the time Eve and I arrive in his Charger to the Jackson Memorial Hospital. The bullet tore through his lung, and it collapsed.

Eve is a mess. I want to comfort her, but I'm still trying to wrap my brain around what happened.

I gave my statement to the cops who arrived, and that helped.

I botched my second attempt to apprehend Leo Fitzgerald. My gut is roiling, and I need to hit something.

But worse is that I can't get it out of my head. No, not Leo. Val's words. *"Does Eve ever talk about it?"*

I sounded like a jerk. Or a fool. *"Talk about what?"*

"The baby."

Yeah, he said *baby*.

I'm pacing, but now, I stop and press a hand against the cold tile of the waiting room. Eve is facing the window, her reflection in the night drawn. She's wrapped her arms around herself.

I'm a jerk, but I just can't…

She was going to have a baby with Val Castillo. And sure, she'd walked out of my life, but—

The doors open and a surgeon walks out into the waiting area. He's wearing scrubs and pulls his cap from his head. "Who's here for Officer Castillo?"

We're not the only ones—a few of the guys from the station are sitting around, but it's Eve who walks up first. She wipes tears from her cheeks. "I am."

I stand away, fold my arms, trying not to be freaked out about the depth of emotion she has for this guy.

"He's out of surgery. We had to resect a portion of his lung, but we were able to stop the bleeding, and barring any complications, he should recover. We have him in intensive care, so contact is limited."

"Can I see him?" Eve asks.

"When he wakes up, you can visit for a few minutes," he says.

She thanks him and he leaves, and a couple of the other officers give her hugs as they leave.

Like she might be his grieving widow.

I know I'm a jerk, but I can't watch so I head to the end of the hall where I find a vending machine. I use my credit card and choose a bag of chips. The wire rings circle, but of course the stupid bag catches on the end.

I give the machine a slam.

It shudders but the bag doesn't move.

A word leaves my lips, but I manage to cut it off before it fully enters public airspace. Still.

I hit the machine again, but the chip bag is glued to the machine.

"Here," Eve says from behind me and presses a bill into the machine. It gobbles it, and she presses the button for the chips.

The ring frees my chips, and hers too and they fall to the

bottom.

She looks at me, no smile, as she reaches in to retrieve them. Hands me my bag.

Admittedly she looks tired, her hair wild from running her hands through it, probably. Her makeup is smudged, and blood still saturates her shirt.

I probably don't look much better, although thankfully, I'm no longer bare chested. One of the docs gave me a scrub shirt after I washed up.

I open my chips. Lean against the wall.

She leans against the other one. Looks at me. "I'm sorry Fitzgerald got away."

I lift a shoulder.

"Rem, you were beating up the vending machine."

I meet her eyes. Swallow, then look away. I don't even know where to start.

She's silent, just the crunching between us.

Finally, "It's not just Fitzgerald, is it?"

"Did you almost marry this guy, Eve?"

She draws in a breath.

"He told me about the baby."

One eyebrow dips down. "Rem. What are you saying? You've known about the baby for years—"

"Did you...did you want—"

"The baby? I don't know, Rem." She throws the unopened bag into the trash (and I have a crazy urge to go after it) and crosses her arms. "I didn't really have much choice after the miscarriage."

Miscarriage.

I draw in a breath. "How far along were you?"

She looks away. "Four months."

I remember her at four months, with Ashley. Remember that

143

the baby started to kick around them.

"I guess I didn't realize you were that far."

"That's why they had to do the emergency surgery. Because the placenta tore away…" She shook her head. "Yes, Rem. I would have had the baby. Had it not died, I would have had it."

"And married Val?"

She lifts a shoulder, looks away. Lifts her hand to her cheek.

I go back to my chips. "How'd it happen?"

She's quiet, frowning. I look up. "The miscarriage."

Her mouth tightens.

"I know you told me, but—"

"Really. How many times do I have to—okay, fine." Eve pauses. "It's your fault, you know. You…you made me feel like we were a team—"

"We were a team."

"So were Val and I."

I've lost my appetite again, the chips churning in my gut. "They why didn't you stay with him—"

"Because he blamed himself, too."

I look at her.

Her jaw tightens. "He didn't know I was pregnant, Rem. If he had, I'm sure, well, he would have stopped me. But I wanted to go with him to confront Hector, and…" She looks away. "It got violent before either of us could stop it. He just…took off. And, pushing me out of the way was, I don't know, reflex maybe. But… yes. That's what killed the baby."

"You fell."

"A flight of stairs, but I landed wrong and—"

"The baby was killed."

"I almost didn't make it." She draws a breath, her hands on her arms. "I guess I didn't tell you that part. I'm sorry."

I'm silent, seeing it all, the truth pruning my anger. "I'm sorry to bring that up again."

"I…" She looks at me. "I'm sorry for leaving Minneapolis. For not saying yes, the first time." She draws in a breath. "I didn't love Val, Rem. He reminded me of you, maybe, but…" She gives me a short, sad smile. "Because of the miscarriage, they said I might never be able to have a child again."

Oh wow.

"And I knew, if I ever wanted a child, I wanted it with you."

"That's why you came back to me."

"Like I said, I didn't love Val. And you coming to Miami… well, I guess I'd been waiting for you for five years to come and get me."

Women. "I don't understand you Eve."

She draws in a breath, and clearly that was the wrong thing to say. So, I try again with, "I'm sorry it took me so long."

I get the smallest nod, as if she might forgive me for not reading her mind. I want to reach out to her, but it feels awkward and maybe a little too late.

One of the officers comes walking down the hallway. "He's awake."

She looks up at me. "I should go in."

I let out a trembling breath, not sure where we stand, the strangest sense that I've lost her, somehow. I have to do something. Get out of here. "I think I should go talk to Helen Fitzgerald. See if I can get another lead on Leo before he completely vanishes."

"Yeah. That's a good idea. But first, you should get a shower. And change. And maybe get some shut-eye."

"You should stay here," I say, not sure why.

She nods.

"But," I say. "I'm coming back for you, Eve. Just in case you're wondering."

And I'm not sure why that was the right answer, but she presses her hands to her face, and I pull her into my arms, holding her. I bend my head, put my voice to her ear and say the words she needs. "I love you. And I'm sorry for the babies you've lost."

We rock for a moment, and then she finally looks up at me. "Go get him, Batman. I'm not going anywhere."

What is it about a woman—the *right* woman—that can turn a spark into a blow torch inside a guy? And she called me Batman, an old nickname from our police days. I don't know why, but hearing it again lights a bonfire in me.

I'm roaring to go as I hit the street in the early morning light. I get an Uber back to the station, grab the Corvette, check into a downtown hotel and shower.

My brain is churning, though. And not just about Fitzgerald.

If I could go back in time, I'd stop Eve from going to Miami, just like she said. And it only takes a moment for me to figure out how.

I'd make sure Booker didn't die, because with him at the helm, Danny doesn't become chief.

And Eve doesn't leave me.

Coulda. Woulda. Shoulda.

By the time I'm out of the shower, staring at the dark press of the wee hours, I realize I'm hours away from landing on the doorstep of some nursing home to demand answers.

I fall face down on the bed for about four hours.

Sleep isn't my friend—you can imagine what I dream about—and I'm up with the first light. Coffee, a muffin in a baggie, and I'm in my convertible, heading to Cyprus Gardens Senior Care Center.

I don't expect a country club, but neither do I expect the nursing home to resemble a strip mall. The long building is painted a deep coral, with a mansard roof and tiny hurricane windows. I park in a lot in desperate need of resurfacing and get out.

Next door is a Dollar Tree, across the street a car wash adds mist to the already humid air. The lot is about half full.

I scoop up the flowers I've picked up on the way at a grocery store, still in their cellophane.

I enter the lobby. It's a friendly place with white tile inlaid with a design of Cyprus trees. A wall of windows behind the office reveals an inner courtyard with a pool.

But the place smells of a nursing home, as if time has slowed, the breath of eternity hovering nearby. And, it's lethally quiet.

A receptionist at the front desk notices me. I approach with that charm Eve mentioned. Her name tag says Brittany. "Hello, Brittany. I'm here to see Helen Fitzgerald. I'm an old friend visiting from Minneapolis, so I forgot to make an appointment. I'm hoping I can drop in?"

I flash my best Minnesota nice smile.

Brittany is young, blonde and cheerful and it occurs to me that she's exactly the kind of person that Leo Fitzgerald would hunt down. I want to tell her to be careful, but I don't want to scare her.

I need to talk to Helen.

Brittany smiles. "Sure. Just let me buzz you in. Helen is in room 110."

I suppose there's not a lot of people trying to break into nursing homes, but the fact that I didn't have to show my I.D. or sign in has me wondering if they'll have any records as to how often Leo visits.

A few doors are open, and I see the beds are two to a room, some of the people in beds, other sitting in chairs or wheelchairs.

I find Helen's room at the end of the first hall, right before a door that opens to a large meeting room.

Her door is half-open, and I knock before I enter. "Helen Fitzgerald?"

She's sitting by the window in a rocking chair, looking out at the pool grounds. The sun is bright against the waters, and the pool is equipped with a number of lifts and a shallow entry.

Helen looks at me and smiles as I walk in.

Her hair is cut into a sleek bob, and she is wearing a white shirt with a chunky necklace, and a skirt, her feet in slippers. "Johnny. What are you doing here?"

I raise an eyebrow. "I'm not Johnny, ma'am."

"Are those for me, Johnny?" She reaches for the flowers.

"Yes," I say, and she gathers them in with such joy I feel a prick of remembered guilt.

Lurking in my brain is a memory of my own mother, back in my original timeline after her first stroke. She lay in her bed, barely responsive, her face twisted, stripped of emotion. I was a terrible son back then.

I silently vow to find them, and make sure I don't repeat my mistakes.

"Can I sit?" I ask, gesturing to another chair.

"Of course, Johnny." She reaches out and pats the chair. "Lenny just left, but he'll be back." Her smile is accompanied by a nod.

I'm not sure if it's dementia or Alzheimer's, but I don't want to jar her. Still, "Ma'am, I'd like to talk to you about your son, Leo."

She is smelling the flowers. "Lenny brings me flowers, sometimes."

"Is that what you call him? Lenny?"

Her gaze flickers up, and she studies me. "He's a good boy."

"I'm sure he is."

Her smile fades. "It's not his fault, you know."

"What's not his fault?"

"He just gets upset. It's from the war." She's earnest now. "He didn't come back the same."

The war. From his military jacket, Leo served in Desert Storm.

She smells the flowers again. "I remember things, you know. Like that time you two took my car." She winks. "You two boys. Always getting into trouble." Her word catches her. "But he's a good boy, my Lenny."

"Helen, did Johnny—did I—go to school with Lenny?"

She laughs. "You wanted to be just like him. I know you did. That's why you joined the army, right?"

I nod.

Her fingers pluck one of the petals of the daisy. "So terrible. Just, terrible." She picks another petal, and this time lets it fall. "So many lives. So many boys, killed." Her voice trembles. "No!"

I catch the flowers as she throws them at me. Oh—

"Stop!" She's yelling now, starting to rise from her chair. "Stop, Johnny! Don't hurt him. Don't—" She looks at me now, her eyes wild. "You are a bad boy. You—you made Lenny cry."

I catch her wrist as she lunges at me. "Helen! It's okay, it's okay."

Then she starts to cry, big weeping breaths. "You did this! You—you made Lenny cry! He trusted you, and you made him cry!"

I catch her just as she crumbles to the floor, weeping, thrashing. "Helen, calm down. Just—"

"What's going on in here?" The door bangs open and I'm not sure if I'm relieved or panicked when an orderly the size of a nose guard enters the room. His badge reads Rico and he crouches before Helen. "Mrs. Fitzgerald, calm down, it's okay."

She's resisting us and he gets up and presses a button by the door. By the time more nurses arrive, Helen is curled into a ball, weeping.

I back up, holding up my hands watching as one of the nurses gives her a sedative. Then I shrink into a corner as they get her into bed. One of the nurses takes her pulse, is speaking to her in low tones.

Rico turns to me. "You gotta leave, man."

No, not yet. I stare at Helen. "Alzheimer's?"

Rico nods.

"I can't leave. I need her help." It's then I pull my badge.

By the tightening of Rico's mouth, I know someone is in trouble.

"Listen, I just need help tracking down her son, Leo. He's a suspect in a number of murders and—"

"Lenny?" Rico is frowning. "Naw—I don't believe it." He gestures with his head toward the door, and he's got a good eighty pounds on me, so I obey.

Besides, I fear Helen's reaction to my words.

I get outside the room. "Do you know him?"

Rico looks down the hall one way, then the next, and finally back to me. "Of course. He's here nearly every week visiting."

"Really?"

"Yeah, man. He's a good son."

Just like Helen said.

"She called me Johnny. Do you know who that might be?"

Rico shakes his head. "Naw. But you're not the first. I think it must be someone her son knew. Nor are you the first person she's freaked out on. The thing is, Alzheimer's patients have this amazing ability to remember the distant past as if it were yesterday. Twenty, thirty, even forty years. They'll describe it as if it just happened. Maybe this Johnny was a childhood friend of her son's."

Johnny.

"Listen. I don't know about any Johnny, but I need to find Leo—Lenny. Do you have an address for him?"

Rico shakes his head. "I don't think so. You can ask, but I think Lenny lives on a boat."

"A boat? Like a houseboat?"'

"No, it's a big trawler. Real pretty, forty-five footer. He docks it at Dolphin Marina, just up the road, toward Fort Lauderdale."

Yes! I manage not to slam my fist into the air, but by the time I get outside, I have Eve on the phone. "I found him."

She sounds tired. "Val is okay. He's awake and talking."

I unlock my door. And, I know how much this means to her, so, "That's good, honey. Real good." I open the door. "But you need some rest. I booked us a room at the Marriott just down the street from the hotel. You can walk there."

She makes a sort of humming sound of agreement.

"Really, babe. You're exhausted."

"Okay. But where are you going?"

"Leo Fitzgerald lives on a *boat*."

"Seriously?"

"Yeah. The Dolphin Marina in Fort Lauderdale." I put the key in, and turn down the radio as REO Speedwagon tells me to take it on the run.

"Rem. Be careful," she says.

"I'm just going to see if he's there. Stake it out. If he is, I'll call for backup."

"Promise."

"Yes. Absolutely." Especially since now Val is permanently in my head, haunting me.

"Okay. I'll go to the hotel."

"Babe. We got him. We *got* him."

"I knew you would, Rem. I love you."

"You too." I hang up and key up the GPS. Then, I crank the volume, letting the wind share the song as I head out to I-95. Appropriately, Journey's "Faithfully" serenades me as I pull out.

We're going to be okay, Eve and me. I get it—the thing with Val. The first time around, I wasn't, in the least, the guy who deserved her. In fact, in those days, it might have been better for her to move on, to find someone who could commit to her, earlier.

Maybe I deserve it, really, fate reminding me that by the grace of God, etcetera, etcetera.

I could get used to life in Florida, maybe. I like the palm trees, the blue skies, the smell of the ocean in the breeze, although I'm not a fan of the heat emanating from the pavement, the congestion of the city, the incessant honking.

We don't honk in Minnesota.

I finally hit the highway and open her up, all the way to the airport, get off and wind myself through back streets until I find myself on a street edged by a half-block of chain link fence.

The gate is open, so I drive in. In the parking lot, all manner of boat sits trailered, from fishing vessels to de-masted sailboats.

I drive into the stretch of street bordering a canal. Boats are docked at a long concrete pier. I pull up and get out, the sun high and bouncing off the white hulls.

There's an office-slash-repair shop located near the entrance, so I head there. Inside, I'm met by a long desk and a young man in a short sleeve collared shirt with a dolphin logo on his chest.

This time I flash my badge. "I'm looking for a guy named Leo—or Lenny—Fitzgerald. His boat is docked here."

The kid—I put him early twenti es, tanned, clean-cut, draws in a breath.

"I don't—"

"He's wanted in suspicion of thirty-eight murders."

This rattles the kid, and he swallows, then nods and heads to the computer. A couple keystrokes, then, "He's in slip 68. At the end of the first pier."

"Thanks." I head back outside, remembering my words to Eve. *"I'm just going to see if he's there. If he is, I'll call for backup."*

Promise.

But first I need to know, right?

I head down the pier, just a guy with a yacht out for a stroll past high-end speed boats, a few trawlers and an occasional sailboat.

I do the math and spot number 68 before I reach it. The boat there is a real beauty—a double-decker cruiser, with a living compartment, a crow's nest, and a railing around the outside. It's in good condition, with lawn chairs and a cooler in the back.

Not unlike the motor homes of the north.

A door, in the back, is closed, something I notice as I walk by.

No movement on the boat, and the urge to go inside is crawling through me.

I blow out a breath and keep walking.

What if he's inside, sleeping?

I continue to the end, and stand there, looking down at the brackish water, my heart thumping.

I promised.

But I can't drag anyone out here if I don't know if he's here, either. I'll just poke around, then go back to the car, grab my cell and call for help.

I turn.

It takes a second for my brain to register, to realize that the materialization of twenty-four years of searching is standing right in front of me, tall, bronzed, wide-shouldered.

And pissed.

I barely see the board he swings at me, certainly not enough to put up my arm, to ward off the blow.

It hits me square on the side of my head.

Then I'm falling, the world spinning, and the last thing I know is the cold grip of water as it pulls me under.

CHAPTER 15

I've been in worse places, I'm sure of it.

I told you I went undercover for the better part of ten years in my original timeline (and the only timeline I really remember) in the Brotherhood, Hassan Abdilhali's organization. It brought me to Duluth, then Madison, and finally Chicago, following the drug trafficking and money laundering into dark places.

Despite the what the movies might suggest, I never tested the drugs, I never broke the law, and I didn't sympathize with the guy I was trying to nail.

But I did get adept at lying, at switching my persona off and on.

And, not panicking when I walked into traps.

But never, in all those years, did I wake up with my wrists tied behind my back, my ankles also bound, dropped like cargo in the back of a boat.

By the feel of it, we've left shore long behind. My skull pounds as if my brains are trying to break free—I'm probably deep in the throes of a concussion—and I'm shivering, a chill born from my soggy clothing, despite the heat of the air.

Or, I could be in even worse shape than that. Impossible to check at the moment.

I lick away the salty mist of the spray the motor is digging up and try and make out my surroundings.

Leo is up on the fly bridge, driving, the sun to the west and dropping, causing his shadow to drape across the stern of the craft. For its part, the sun isn't going down easily, its fight leaving a scrape of bloody orange across the sky.

I force myself to sit up, wince and look over the edge.

Land is in the far distance, a tiny ripple of dark in the west.

I stifle a word and lay back. Perfect.

I can only guess that I've been out for hours. But I'm not dead, my body alligator fodder, so that bodes well.

Or not. Because in my gut, I know what's happening, don't you?

Leo is going to give me a watery send off, out in the deep ocean where I'll never be found.

Sorry, Eve.

And no, Val, I guess I haven't figured out how to walk away.

But this isn't over. I'm tied with rope, and he probably knows his knots, so my best bet is to cut them, but in this dim light, I see nothing but soft edges. A cooler, a couple fishing rods.

A lifejacket.

I pick it up and manage to drop it overboard, an orange neon breadcrumb. Just in case anyone misses me.

Then, I start to wiggle my wrists, moving them back and forth, my palms up and down. The rope has give. I just need to work that give to my advantage.

The motor cuts, and the boat slows, my heartbeat suddenly deafening. I continue to work my hands.

Leo comes down the ladder and lands on the back deck. He's

dressed in a pair of shorts and a loose linen shirt and flip flops, like he's on vacation and we're out for a sundowner.

I can't take my gaze off his tattoo, the one on his arm with two hands folded together, bound with barbed wire.

He looks at me, takes a breath and there's something in his eyes I don't understand.

Almost, confusion. He walks over and opens his cooler and pulls out a beer, pops the top and tosses it into a nearby trash bin. Sits on his armchair and takes a drink.

He looks out toward the sunset a long time before he speaks.

Meanwhile, I've created a tiny gap in my bonds.

"I like to come out here, when I'm not on the road," he says softly. "It's so quiet. Peaceful. All the shouting in my brain gets turned off."

It's like we're buddies, sharing a moment.

"What shouting?"

He takes another drink, then looks at me. "I didn't recognize you at first. I mean, I barely saw you last night, but when you walked right by me on the dock, heading to my boat, I knew." He points his bottle at me. "The bar, in Montrose. You accused me of killing my girlfriend, Lauren. We got into a scrape."

I nod.

He's looking at me. "Who are you?"

I want to say something deep and ominous like, *your destiny*, but I go for the truth. "A cop."

"And you've been dogging me for over twenty years for a crime I didn't commit?" He takes another drink, gets up and turns his back on me.

He's that trusting that he can take me. That I'm not going to jump him.

Well, probably not, at this rate.

"You killed Lauren Delaney because she broke up with you, didn't you? You waited until she got off work, then chased her down, tackled her, held her down and strangled her. Left her a tip."

He doesn't move.

"And then sweet Gretchen Anderson. I met her, you know, after our fight. She was an ER nurse. Pretty, I can see why you went for her. What happened, Leo? Did she break up with you too?"

With his back to me, I've been able to move my shoulders, create more gap. I have enough play in the rope to run my palms together, up and down. Gotta keep him talking.

"I loved Gretchen," he says quietly, still looking out into the night. "She broke up with me because of you."

I didn't expect that, and the emotion in his words hits me. I'm not sure what to be afraid of—the cool, detached serial killer, or the man driven by emotion.

Probably both.

"I met her the first time my mother fell. Brought her into the ER, and Gretchen was there." He takes a breath. "She was pretty."

"And yet you stalked her after work, and again, chased her down, and strangled her, and—"

"I didn't kill her!" He turns now, and even in the fading sunlight, I can see the spark in his eyes.

I keep my voice even. "We found your DNA on her."

"Of *course* you did. Because we…" His mouth tightens. "After you jumped me, I went to see her. It was late, and she'd already seen what I did to you, and it scared her."

Aw, c'mon, I wasn't that roughed up, but his gaze is hard in mine.

"It took me a month to get her to go out with me again. We went out and…and afterwards, I brought her home. I didn't find out she was dead until a few days later."

My hand is stuck about half-way out of the ropes.

"I didn't do nothing to either of those girls," he says and drops his empty beer into the trash. Looks at me. "You gotta stop following me." Then he takes a step toward me.

I kick at him, scooting back, my hands still stuck. "Who's shouting?"

He recoils, puts his hand to his head, shakes it.

"Leo. Who is shouting at you?"

"Johnny!"

His eyes are wild, and he takes a breath. "Johnny."

"Who's Johnny?" Nearly free. Just a little more tug.

He presses his hands to his head now. "Stop."

"Leo—"

"Stop!"

"Is Johnny telling you what to do right now? Is Johnny here?" And I'm suddenly remembering Helen's words. *He didn't come back the same.*

Maybe Leo has a split personality, something brought on by war.

"No, he's not here!" He snaps, but he's still holding his head.

"Okay, okay." I soften my voice. "Is that why you moved to Florida? To get away from Johnny?"

He stares at me, and for a moment, the fury clears. "This is all his fault."

The blood has started circulating in my right hand, pinpricking my fingers. "Why?"

"It was his idea to—" He clamps his mouth shut. Shakes his head. "It got out of control."

"What got out of control?"

He stands up and reaches into his shirt pocket, pulls out some smokes. His hand is trembling as he pulls out a cigarette, puts the pack back, then grabs a lighter from his shorts and lights it.

For the first time, I see that he wears a thick ring on his right hand.

A thin trail of smoke trickles into the air. "It was just a theory, okay? Just a game we played when we were drinking."

He takes another drag. "What if we kidnapped the principal, how would we do it? What if we robbed a bank, how would we do it? What if we stole a car..." He looks at me, lowers his voice. "What if we bombed a building?"

I still. Wait—*what?*

He takes a long pull on his cigarette, as if waiting for me to catch up. I have. "Leo, what job did you have in the military?"

"I was on a combat team—breaching and demolition." He holds my gaze.

"So you know bombs."

"Had an entire notebook on different kinds of bombs chemistries. And my own designs. I loved it." He nods, takes another drag. "Or I used to. I threw them away after...well—"

"After the coffee shop bombings," I finish for him. "Leo, you made those bombs, didn't you?"

His cigarette is a bright orange bullseye as the night deepens. "Like I said, I thought it was a game."

"C'mon, Leo, you're smarter than that, aren't you? When Vega hired you, you knew he was going to use them."

"Vega didn't hire me."

Silence, and paper crackles. Then, "It was Johnny's idea. He delivered the bombs. Even stuck around to make sure they went off."

Sure he did. Except I saw *Leo* at CityPerk. At least in my, um, dream.

With my hand numb, I can force it through the bonds,

crushing my thumb into my palm. I'm not sure it's dislocated, but I grit my teeth against a sudden thrush of pain.

But my hands are free.

The blood rushes in, and I nearly cry aloud with it.

Leo is quietly finishing off his smoke.

"So, this is Johnny's fault," I say. "He probably killed the girls, too."

He looks up at me, and his eyes widen. "Yeah. Johnny killed them."

If Leo was in demolition, it's a sure bet he saw guys he cared about get killed. Which might lead to a psychotic break.

Even a split personality.

"Why did Johnny make you cry," I say quietly.

His gaze tears away from me, and he shakes his head.

"Who is Johnny, Leo?"

"Johnny is my friend," he says and throws the cigarette away, into the night. He gets up. "You need to leave us alone."

He takes two strides toward me.

"Why did he make you cry, Leo?"

He doesn't stop. Okay, here we go. I rear back and kick him. He practically slaps my kick away, reaches down and hauls me up.

But he doesn't know my hands are free. I swing them between his grip and break his hands apart, then slam my palm into his chin.

His head bounces back, and he curses.

Cuffs me with a right-handed cross.

I'm falling, my feet still tied, my balance off.

He grabs me from behind, but I slam an elbow into him. He grunts, I turn and land a right hook.

He's bleeding from the mouth and spits blood.

"Why did you cry, Leo?" I need my feet free. I stagger back, against the stern bench and scrabble to untie my feet.

He's leaning over, breathing hard. A line of blood drips from his mouth. Then he looks up at me, and the look in his eyes turns my blood cold. "Because Johnny killed Julia."

I'm stymied, my mind racing through the known cases on the board, searching for that name. But I've been jumping through so many worlds, I don't know.

Leo rushes me. I still don't have my feet untied, but I put up hands for protection.

Like I said, Leo is big. He gets his arms all the way around my legs, lifting me like he might be about to body slam me.

And then, just like that, he dumps me over the side of the boat.

But not quite. Because I have a hold of his shoulders, and even as I fall, I grip onto him.

We splash like bricks into the ocean. I manage a breath before I go under, push him away, and have to kick like a porpoise to get my head above the water.

I gasp and pull in a breath as I spot Leo under water. He surfaces next to me, and turns, aiming for the boat.

Oh, no you don't. I grab his leg, nearly get kicked, and pull him down.

One of us is going to die, and it's not going to be me.

The problem with water is that it slows everything. My punches are futile, hitting Leo as if I'm wearing my gloves, and I'm like a rock, sinking fast. He hits me, too—his jabs are more effective, and my nose smarts.

The need for air razors my lungs, and I push him away, and struggle for the surface.

I break free and lap up air, searching. The boat has floated away, a good fifteen feet in the current.

Leo has vanished.

I don't even have time to swear. Hands grab me from behind and push me down. His arm vices my neck, and I'm struggling, clawing, punching his face.

He knows his rear naked choke holds, and in a moment, my vision, despite the blackness, is lighting with the flare of panic.

No air.

We're sinking, fast, his body dead weight.

I get my hand up, between his grip and my neck, but now a burst of white blinds me.

I hear the curse, deep in my brain, because I'm going to die. Right here in the dark freakin' ocean.

I'm really thrashing now, using up the rest of my air, fighting, and it's enough to wiggle free.

Maybe he's running out of air, too.

I manage to turn around and my fist hits something hard. But it doesn't matter.

I'm out of air and I've got nothing left.

And strangely, Gene Latsky is in my head. *You think you'll catch him?*

Yeah, I did. I really did.

CHAPTER 16

I'd always known I would die this way, falling into the depths of some body of water, the breath siphoned out of me, my body a leaden weight.

I dreamed it, after all.

In my dream—or maybe this is real—I'm reaching for something, an indistinct light, a voice that echoes faintly in the water, the sense I've left something behind.

But the voice and light are fading, and all I'm left with is a thump of my heartbeat, like a fist pounding against my rib cage.

It's that thump, this time a punch, that causes me to gasp, that yanks my body from the briny depths and propels me to life.

I open my eyes and gulp in a desperate breath.

"He's back," says a voice.

I'm coughing, my throat fills and I roll over, expelling the ocean hard from my lungs. My body is wracking, and I flop back like a dead fish.

Everything hurts.

Least of which is the fact that Leo got away.

It's dark, but in the dim glow of floodlights I make out men in wetsuits standing over me, another man in uniform.

He peels a pair of defibrillator pads from my chest and a second later another man presses his stethoscope to my pecs.

"Rembrandt!" My name issues from a deep baritone, a voice I know but don't expect and as my vision clears, I'm looking for him.

"Burke?" I manage and the guy with the defib patches looks up, then makes room for my best friend to crouch next to me. "What in the devil are you doing here?"

We're on the stern of a large vessel, the deck slick and wet. Burke is wearing a stripped expression and puts his hand on my shoulder. "You scared us to death."

Us. He looks up, and so do I.

Eve is standing in the dim glow of light, her hands over her mouth, shaking.

Us.

"Eve—"

"You promised me!" She clamps her hands over her mouth again, probably so that nothing terrible releases. She's shaking her head, horror in her eyes.

I'm not completely guilty, but you saw my intent. I push myself up, feeling a shooting pain deep in my sternum.

Ah. CPR. That's nice.

"What happened?"

"Before or after you broke your promise to me," Eve snaps.

I look at her, then to Burke. "What *happened?*"

"Eve figured out where you might have been taken, and we followed the EPIRB signal on the life jacket."

That was me, thank you.

"We saw you in the water right before you went down for the last time. You can thank the Coast Guard guys for pulling you out of the drink and saving your life."

He motions at the guys in wetsuits. I give them a nod.

But it's a hollow victory without Leo. I shake my head. "He hit me from behind, tied me up. Got me out on the boat. I can't believe he got away, again."

Burke gives a tiny shake of his head. "We got him, Rem. Leo Fitzgerald is alive and handcuffed, and secured in quarters."

I take a breath. "What?"

"Yeah. While these guys were saving your life, we took a boarding team and caught up to Fitzgerald before he could get away."

"You got him."

"He's not going anywhere, pal."

I press my hand to my face, feeling a little like Eve. Overwhelmed, and in disbelief.

We got him.

We got him!

The Coast Guard guys have given us space, and now I try and get up, but my body is shaking.

Eve crouches beside me and puts her arms around me, helping.

We fall as the boat picks up speed, but that's okay. I hold her, and for a long moment we shake together.

"I'm only forgiving you because you decided to live," Eve says. I meet her eyes, and she's not kidding.

"Okay," I say and kiss her.

My heartbeat is thundering, my body jiggering and I can't help but feel like somehow, I missed the climax of this epic story.

Whatever. Leo is in custody. The nightmare is over.

I lean away. "How did Burke get here?"

"He called me shortly after you did, and I told him what you were doing. He got on a plane."

I look at Burke, and he lifts a shoulder. "I know you."

Apparently.

"I checked in with Eve after I landed, and when she said she hadn't heard from you—"

"I was busy."

"I called you five times."

"I was probably napping in the back of Leo's boat."

At this, Eve leans back and looks at my head. "Oh, Rem. You have a wicked goose-egg."

"And my brain is still trying to punch its way out of my skull."

I've scared her. "Just kidding."

"Hardly." Her mouth is tight.

"We drove out to the marina," Burke continues, "but Leo's boat was gone. That's when Eve did some sleuthing."

"It wasn't hard. I tracked the boat on Marine Traffic, and saw him heading out to sea, and I had a hunch."

I grin at her. "Really."

"An *educated guess*. Nothing that involves body parts."

"Mmmhmm," I say.

"We saw you go overboard, and that's when the Coast Guard guys suited up," Burke says. "We probably need to get back into the gym." He grins.

"Anytime, bro."

Eve climbs off me, and I find my feet, grabbing onto the rail.

"You okay?"

"Woozy."

"We're getting your skull x-rayed when we get to shore."

"I'm fine. I want to talk to Leo."

"No. Let's just let both of you cool off a bit." Burke says. He throws a towel at me, and I wrap up in it.

I sit on a bench next to Eve, the wind whipping around me, and stare into the darkness.

The sea at night is wild and mysterious, the moon tipping the wave peaks in silver, stars falling into the horizon. I can't help but think about what lies beneath, and how easily I might be, right now, lost.

As it is, I have too many questions stirring in my head to sit in quiet triumph.

"He is our mysterious bomb-maker," I say to Eve.

She's been leaning against me and now sits up. "What?"

"Yeah. He confessed to making the bombs that took out the two coffee shops."

Her mouth opens.

"It's makes sense, right? Because before, the killings had stopped—and he was there, so maybe he got blown up."

She stares at me, a deep frown etched into her brow. It takes me a moment to realize I've just spoken my time travel history aloud.

"What did you say?" she says slowly, and glances at the bump on my head. I'm hoping she thinks it's the concussion talking.

I swallow and reach for another subject. "He kept talking about this guy named Johnny. I think it might have been his accomplice."

"What accomplice? You think the Jackson killings were done by two people?"

"No. It's just, he didn't sound completely irrational."

"Most psychopaths don't. That's what makes them so terrifying. They're not overtly crazy. And we've already established that the Jackson killer is organized. He finds his prey and hunts them down. Leaves them with a twenty-dollar bill, marking his kill."

"Then what was this? He beat me over the head and was going to drop me into the sea."

"Panic?" Burke says, standing against a pole not far away. "You always say every murderer makes a mistake."

I look away. I don't know what has me rattled. "Everything fits, right? Leo's military background, his tattoo, his DNA on Lauren and Gretchen."

"Did he say anything about the twenties he leaves?"

I shake my head. Bad idea. I wince and put my hand to it, as if to hold my brains in place.

"The smell they talk about—maybe it's because he wears the same clothes for every attack. You know, a sort of disguise," Burke says. "We searched his truck and found soiled clothing in his bag. Smelled pretty rank."

"That could just be from a week on the road," Eve says suddenly, and I frown at her.

"What? I'm just saying, we need more than smelly clothes to connect him. Especially since he's been living in Florida for over a decade. I need to connect the murders, and the time of death with his routes, see if I can establish his presence in Minnesota."

Yeah, that's bothering me, too.

And, "He said that Johnny had killed someone named Julia. I've been thinking through the victims—do you remember a Julia?"

Eve shakes her head, looks at Burke. He's frowning. "No."

"So, does that make thirty-nine?" I ask.

"Maybe one of the victims went by a different name."

"Funny that he even knew their names, right? I mean—do you remember the people who wait on you in a restaurant? Or a bar?"

"Maybe I do if I'm going to kill them," Burke says.

We're nearing shore, the lights of the city pricking against the darkness.

"There's something his mother said—did I mention she has dementia? And Leo visits her every week. She kept calling me Johnny."

"You think this Johnny is a real guy?" Eve says.

"She said that Johnny made Lenny—that's our guy—cry. And when I asked him, he said Johnny killed Julia."

Silence from my cohorts.

The boat is slowing.

"When did he kill her?"

"I don't know. Could be one of the victims in the yard. Or... someone else?" The dock is coming into view. Good. I need to get my legs back on solid ground. "She said Johnny joined the military because Leo did. Leo's an only child, otherwise I would have thought it was a sibling. But what if Leo had a real friend named Johnny? Maybe he got killed over in Desert Storm?"

We're pulling up to the dock.

"Maybe we should check if there's a Johnny in his platoon," Eve says.

"Let's find out. Might be helpful for questioning. Maybe help us sort truth from fiction."

"And he's wearing a ring," Eve says. "Didn't Meggie Fox mention that?"

She's observant, and it's just another thing I love about her.

"Could be a class ring. Maybe high school?" Burke says.

"I'll take a look at it." Eve writes it down in her phone.

I'm standing in the back when I spot police on the dock, waiting to take Leo into custody. I glance at Burke. "And we need to extradite him back to Minnesota."

"Already have the paperwork," he says. "But it's not going to be easy. He shot a cop."

"We need to get him on a plane, pronto," I say and Burke nods.

A couple of Coast Guard guys bring Leo out from below deck, and he spots me.

His eyes are dark, his mouth tight. "How many lives do you have?" he says as he comes up on deck.

"I've lost count," I say, meeting his eyes. "But yours is done."

Leo spits at me as they wrestle him off the boat. Burke follows behind, probably to fight with the bureaucrats.

"I'd feel much better if we got your head looked at," Eve says.

She's not going to find anything but relief there.

We got the Jackson killer.

The nightmare is over.

CHAPTER 17

I want my own bed. In my own house. With my own car.
I want my own life back.

These are my thoughts as I roll over and stare at the popcorn ceiling in Eve's old bedroom at the Mulligan house.

I've slept like the dead for the last fourteen hours after getting X-rayed in Miami (no skull fracture) and hopping a plane with a cuffed and angry Leo Fitzgerald in tow. (He owes us his life after we extradited him from the Miami police who were thirsty for blood.) We arrived at the Mulligans late in the evening, and I went straight to bed.

After being jacked up on adrenaline for that long, I dropped like a stone. I'm groggy, strung out, achy and still in glorious disbelief.

We got him.

The Jackson killer.

Eve isn't in the bed next to me, and a look out the window says the morning has come and gone. The sun is high, the lake a deep blue, and it's a good day to be alive.

I'm debating my next move—coffee, sleep or tracking down

Eve—when my cell phone vibrates on the bedside stand. I pick it up.

Shelby.

"Aren't you supposed to be nursing a baby or something?"

"I would be if Mayor Vega didn't keep harassing me. What's the deal? According to her she's called you no less than eight hundred and thirty-seven times."

I look at my phone. "Eleven."

"Close enough. Answer her, for Pete's sake."

"I got back late and had my phone on Do Not Disturb."

"You're the chief of police. You're not supposed to be going on field trips to Miami."

"Hey. I brought in the Jackson killer." Sort of. I mean, I had help, but let me enjoy the moment.

"Kudos to you on that. I'll bet that's what the mayor is going to say too."

I'll bet not, how about you? But I don't say that to Shelby.

"I'm sure. Right after she lays into me for the news article—"

"Which saved a life."

I prop my arm over my eyes. My head still throbs, thank you, Leo.

"I think she just wants an update, and so do I, really. Have we gotten a ballistics report back on Zeke's shooting? Does it match any of the Malakov weapons?"

"Don't you have lackeys for this?"

"You're my lackey. Find out something."

Sheesh, I liked her better as a pharmaceuticals rep. "Aren't you supposed to be on leave?"

"Answer your ding-dang phone, or I'm sending Burke over there."

"Go change a diaper or something."

She hangs up on me.

I sit up, then push to my feet and look out the window. This is my life. And maybe Ashley is gone forever—and I'm still not quite able to breathe through that thought—but at least one nightmare is over.

And I'm the chief of police. Whattya know.

I take a shower, down a few acetaminophens and head downstairs. The kitchen is empty, but I spot Danny in his office, on his computer. He looks up at me. "Rembrandt."

I walk over. "Do you know where Eve is?"

"She left a couple hours ago. Said to tell you to go back to bed."

"She's not the boss of me," I say, and Danny raises an eyebrow because we both know she is.

"Sams said that he scheduled a moving company to empty your house. He wants you and Eve to go over and take out anything else you want before they put things in storage. He wants to start tearing down the burned half by the end of the week."

"I'll tell Eve." I lean against the door frame. "He knows how to get stuff done."

Danny smiles. "Yeah, well, I've been busy too. I got information back from your near hit and run."

It's Ramses Vega, I feel it in my bones. Or, that could just be just anger talking.

"The plates are stolen, but I did manage to get a picture of the car from a local bank on the corner of Highway 7 and Minnetonka Boulevard. They have shots of their parking lot, and the highway, and I did the math and—"

"How long have you been retired?"

"Not long enough. Look." He hands me a printed picture of the man in the car. I can't make out a clear image. The man is wearing a baseball cap, a long sleeve shirt, but he looks white, and maybe middle-aged.

"Not a great help."

"No, but we'll get him."

I hand him back the photo. "It doesn't look like Ramses Vega."

"I interviewed Vega personally. He has an alibi and corroboration. He was checking in with his parole officer."

Of course he was. "Thanks, Danny."

"We'll get him, Rem. It's only a matter of time." He gives me a smile.

It feels good to have Danny Mulligan in my corner. Like another victory.

I raid the fridge, and settle on a banana, then call Zeke. His phone goes to voicemail. "Hey. It's Rembrandt. Just checking on you. I was hoping to talk to you about the shooting. Call me back."

Then I dial Eve.

"What are you doing out of bed?"

"Calm down, Florence." She doesn't laugh. "Listen, Mayor Vega has called me a couple trillion times and I need answers before she calls me back."

"What kind of answers?"

"Did we get a ballistics report back on Zeke?"

"Just a second." She puts me on hold and I walk out to the porch, sit on the steps and watch the waves. The lake is calm today, no dark thunderheads overhead, no stiff wind from the east.

It just might be a beautiful night, too. My gaze goes to the dock.

"Yes. The bullet came from a Beretta M9."

"Really? A 9mm? Huh."

"Why?"

"Oh, I did some reading on Malakov's gang, their weapon of

choice is a .45 ACP."

"So, not Malakov's crew."

I finish off the banana. "I'm going to talk to Zeke, see if we can get any more information out of him about the driver, the car—"

"Rem—"

"If you want, you can meet me at the hospital."

Silence. "Fine. And then I'm taking you home."

"It's going to be a pretty night out. Warm. Perfect for skinny—"

"I'm hanging up now." And she does.

I smile. Because this is my life.

I call an Uber, then get up and go back inside, throw away the banana peel, say goodbye to Danny and am waiting outside when the car pulls up.

I need to score me new wheels, so I scroll through my phone looking at cars as my driver turns on the radio.

He gets a five-star review for his selection; 38 Special comes on with "Back Where You Belong."

We pull up to Methodist Hospital and I know my way to Zeke's room.

Eve is already there, talking with Zeke, and a man with a face I now recognize, Gene Latsky. He wears a white jacket over his dress pants, a tie, and he's got his hands shoved into his pockets, also laughing.

"What did I miss?" I ask.

"I was telling them about eating conch fritters in Miami," Eve says.

I give her a look.

"Yeah, that's the face." She's grinning. And reaches out for my hand.

"How are you, Zeke?" He looks significantly better, his face less drawn.

"Ready to go home. Frankie's picking me up in an hour or so. I'll be at Burke and Shelby's party tonight."

I nod because I'm sure Eve knows about it. I'm in safe hands.

"I just wanted to check in with him before he took off," Gene says. "I'll see you in a couple weeks, then."

Zeke nods and Gene shakes his hand, then looks at me. "Eve said you took a pretty good whack on the old noggin."

"It was worth every bolt of pain." I give him a grim smile. "We caught the Jackson killer."

His eyes widen. "Really?"

"Yep. Remember that guy from the bar so many years ago?"

"Lenny?"

"Yeah. His real name is Leo Fitzgerald. He was holed up in Florida. Worked as a trucker—he'd swing by here on his routes and...well, yeah, we got him."

"I'm still putting together his timeline, corroborating his routes with the murders," Eve says. "I'll have the report done tomorrow, definitely before his arraignment."

Fitzgerald is right now sitting in temporary lockup down at the city jail.

"Wow." Gene nods. "That's tremendous." He hesitates, then. "Rem, I have to tell you, that after we talked, I started thinking. I mentioned he was in the military, right? So I called around, and a couple of my buddies knew him. They have quite a story—said this guy was real popular with the local ladies, if you know what I mean. Used to leave them twenty-dollar tips with the words, *thank you for your service* written on the bill. Got to be a sort of thing with his platoon, a joke. You know, because that's what everybody said to us when we came stateside."

I'm staring at him. "You sure they were talking about Fitzgerald?"

"I think so."

"Do you have their names? I'd like to contact them."

"Sure. No problem. I'll send you their contact information."

Eve has tightened her grip in mine.

We got him.

"Thanks, Gene," I say, and reach over the bed to shake his hand.

He shakes mine, and I notice he's wearing a ring.

"Nice ring," I say.

"Yeah, it's a state champion ring," he says. "Section A champs, football, class of '84." He grins. "I know, silly. But you never forget your high school glory days."

He says goodbye and leaves.

Eve turns to me. "A class ring."

"You think that's the ring Leo was wearing."

"If we can find his school, maybe we can see if this Johnny is real."

"We've got him, Eve. Did you hear what Gene said about the twenties? I'll interview these guys and…this is over."

She's nodding, but wears the strangest look.

"What?"

"His shoe size. It's a fourteen. The print from Hollie and Lauren is from a twelve."

"Are you sure? Maybe it was smudged?"

"Maybe. I'll take another look. But, Rem …" She pauses and holds my gaze for a long time before finishing. "What if Leo isn't the guy?"

Not a chance. I've been following Leo Fitgerald for three lifetimes. "It's him Eve. I know it." I turn to Zeke.

"Listen. I need you to think hard about the shooting. Someone tried to run me over a couple days ago, and we're wondering if there's a connection. Do you remember what kind of car he was in?"

Zeke makes a face, shakes his head. "It was black?"

"Luxury car?"

"Maybe. I'm sorry, Rem. I don't remember. Why?"

"We got the ballistics report back—it's from a 9mm Beretta."

"Malakov's crew carries .45 automatics."

"Yep."

"So, not a cop shooting," Eve says. "I suppose that's a relief."

"It doesn't help us figure out who bombed my Porsche."

"C'mon, tough guy. One case solved per day." Eve pulls me away.

"Is that a rule? A vitamin?"

"A warning. Back to bed, pal."

I raise an eyebrow and turn up the corner of my mouth. "That sounds like a promise."

She winks, but the reality is we're living at her parents' house and by the time we arrive, Bets is making dinner. "I know you were going to have Burke and Shelby's baby shower at your house, but since it's...well..."

"Rubble is the word I think you're looking for, Mom," Eve says.

"Right. Anyway, I asked if they might want to have it here."

She's made a cake and potato salad, and Danny is outside at the grill, and maybe I am ready for a party.

Because Jackson is buttoned up, and I don't hate this plane of existence. If this is my only choice, I'm in. This is my life.

I change (and ignore another call from Mayor Vega, yes, I know, but I'll talk to her in the morning) and help haul food outside to the picnic table.

Burke and Shelby arrive before sunset, toting little Daphne.

Sams is here, with new plans for the house, which Eve dives into, with promises to stop by in the morning.

I knew remodeling was in our future. Fate won't be completely bested.

The smell of burgers scents the summer night, and I'm close to thievery by the time Zeke and Frankie finally show up. She's carrying a gift bag. I think it's for Shelby, but she walks over to me. "I found this. I want you to have it."

I take it, look inside. It's a small box. "What is it?"

She smiles, and again the resemblance to Booker is simply uncanny. It's like having him in the room.

"It's his watch," she says. "I found it in his belongings."

The watch. *The* watch. I look at her, and a strange feeling rushes through me, something almost akin to panic. My throat dries and I swallow. Eke out a "Thank you."

And then I carefully bring the bag inside, to my room and set it on the bedside table like the bomb it is.

Because, *this* is my life.

The night settles around us as we eat and open gifts, a beautiful lavender twilight that blankets the horizon. I'm polishing off my second burger, sitting on the steps of the porch, when Burke walks over to me.

Sits down.

I look over at him. "Why aren't you assembling your Babyzen Yoyo six stroller—"

"What even is that? I mean, if you can't say the words, should you be putting your baby in it?"

I laugh. "How is fatherhood?"

He looks at Shelby, rocking Daphne. "Terrifying."

I smile. "Uh huh."

"And amazing. And tiring and, did I mention terrifying?"

My gaze goes to Eve. She's sitting on a lawn chair, and she's smiling. No, nearly glowing.

Something is different about her. Maybe it's the fact that we've stopped a killer.

But for a moment, I'm in the kitchen with her, my arms around her as we stand at the window and watch our daughter—my Ashley, the one I know, the one who, just a few weeks ago asked me to find her stuffed bear, Gomer.

My throat tightens, and I look away before my eyes water.

This is my life. And Ashley will never be in it.

"I'm thinking of leaving the force," Burke says quietly.

I look at him. "What?"

"It's just—after seeing what happened to you, and Booker, leaving behind Frankie—there's just so much at stake, man. I just can't…" He looks at me. "You get it, right?"

And oddly, I'm right where Booker was, so many years ago. Panicking at the loss of my best detective. *Coward.*

Maybe he's a coward if he *doesn't* face his feelings. If he doesn't look at life in the face and see what he has at stake.

I look at Burke. "Yep. I get it."

He sighs. "I thought you were going to really give it to me."

"Nope."

He says nothing for a long time. Then, "I love ya, Rem."

I look at him, but he gets up and walks away.

Yeah, me too, Burke.

Daphne is fussing, and it's getting late so we pack up dinner, and Burke and Shelby leave, then Zeke and Frankie.

I don't tell Eve about Burke's decision. Not yet.

And I'm not even going to look at the gift bag.

I don't need the watch. Because, *this* is my life.

I'm stuffing a bag full of wrapping paper when she comes out of the house, barefoot, empty handed. "Lemme help." She holds the bag and I finish cleaning, then she ties it.

I'm about to carry it to the trash when she takes my hand. "Rem. I have to tell you something."

I turn to her.

The moonlight transforms her eyes to gold, starlight in her smile. I am a lucky man. And maybe about to get luckier. "Yeah?"

She waits a beat, then, "I'm pregnant."

I still, and my mouth opens.

"Rem?" She presses her hands to my chest. "You're breathing funny."

"No—I'm...oh..." I *am* breathing funny. "I think I need to sit down."

She looks genuinely worried as I walk over to the picnic table and sit on the bench. "Rem?"

"How did this happen?"

She laughs. "Really?"

"I mean—when?"

"I don't know. Sometime in the last month, I guess. The fertility shots worked."

Shots? But it doesn't matter. I rub my hands over my face.

"You look worried."

Of course I'm worried. I mentioned the miscarriages, and Eve is...well, high risk, at the least.

Still. *Pregnant.* I take her hands, pull them to myself. "We're going to have a baby."

For the first time, a flash of fear hues her eyes. "I hope."

I pull her tight. "It's going to be okay, Eve. Everything is going to be okay." I kiss her, and she folds into me, believing me.

And you can feel it too, right?

Everything is going to be okay.

I can live with this life. These changes. The taste of hope back in my chest.

We find ourselves upstairs in her dark bedroom, and she's giggling. "We need our own house."

And how.

But we're noiseless, and after, I pull her into my arms, spooning. "Tomorrow we get our own place."

"Frankie says she has a friend who has a place we can rent. I'm going to meet her in the morning, and we'll go check it out."

I kiss her neck. She tastes of home, and peace and maybe happiness isn't a person, but a choice.

I fall hard, and again sleep like a rock, and it takes the third ring before I wake to Eve shaking me. "Your phone, Rem."

Light dents the shadows, morning upon me. I roll over, swipe it up and press it to my ear. "Chief Stone," I groan.

"Sorry, Chief, but I didn't know who else to call. Detective Burke isn't picking up his phone."

"Who is this?"

"It's Officer Jackson. Sir, um...I don't know how to say this."

Eve's shoulder is curving under the golden light of dawn. I draw my finger down it. "Just spit it out."

"Leo Fitzgerald...he...well, he escaped, boss. He's gone."

CHAPTER 18

Leo Fitzgerald is a slippery sucker.

It's not easy to escape from jail, especially in a city. You're conspicuous, and even if you hide well, the likelihood of someone turning you in is high.

Unless you know how to hide, to blend in. To evade police.

I'm standing in my office, the door closed because I needed just a moment to think before calling the mayor with an update.

Again.

I run my hand over my forehead, staring at the darkened sky, turning bullet gray with the oncoming rainstorm, the clouds pregnant with doom.

The case has been turned over to the Fugitive Task Force, but because Fitzgerald wasn't yet indicted, and still in holding, the U.S. Marshals Service hasn't stepped in.

I've explained all this to Mayor Vega no less than six times today, along with the fact that we've deployed nearly the entire force to find him.

"It's been almost ten hours, Inspector."

"Chief, and I know, Ms. Mayor. We're doing everything we

can to find him."

I called for a perimeter nearly the minute my feet hit the floor, Officer Jackson still outlining how they think he escaped.

"I just don't understand how he got out."

"According to our investigation, he called the guard, saying he was sick around one a.m. He then overpowered him, used the guard's own taser to incapacitate him, got his key card and used that to get into the control center."

"Where was the other guard?"

"Patrol. But we found him also tasered, gagged, then suffocated with a medical waste bag, just like the guard."

"That's horrible."

She has no idea. Young cops, they both left behind wives.

The worst part is, there's another running theory that says Leo had an accomplice, someone who got into the control room and turned off the cameras. The digital recording is blank, even before the guard entered Leo's cage.

We haven't gotten anything useful from any of the other prisoners being held in the block. And, like I said, no camera footage.

"I'm going to say this again, ma'am—we need to alert the public. He's dangerous, and the best way to catch him is to let people know we're looking for him."

"And terrify everyone even more? Stone, your last stunt had my office fielding calls from terrified constituents for two days."

I'm glad I'm not in the same room, given the tone of her voice. "Tell people to stay in their homes, and should they see anyone matching his description, then to call us."

"Not yet," she says, and I close my eyes, pinching the bridge of my nose.

My headache is back.

"Not until we know he's breached the perimeter you've set."

I sigh.

"Give me an update every hour," she says, like I haven't been doing that. She hangs up before I can reply.

The task force has assembled in a conference room just down the hall, and I walk out of my office, heading back to the bullpen.

Reagan is at his desk and looks up. "Your wife dropped this by, sir." He hands me a manila envelope, and I open it.

Inside is the sketch I ordered of Meggie's attacker. I take it out and look at it.

I've always had a hard time seeing a likeness from a sketch, and even now, it really doesn't look like Fitzgerald, to my way of thinking. It's not in color, and the eyes are too far apart, the jaw wider, too. But it does look familiar, so it must be right.

I give it back to Reagan. "Put this on my desk."

I grab another cup of coffee—this might be number twelve—at the coffee station near the door, then walk over and survey the current leads. The task force has made a list of all of Leo's former employers, known contacts and military buddies, and is checking in with all of them.

On another board is a tentative timeline of his escape. It goes blank after 1:47 a.m., although the bodies weren't found until after the five a.m. shift change.

Nearly a three-hour window.

Burke is looking at a map of the city, a red perimeter outlining our estimated border, although, frankly, it could be hours off.

He's holding a cup of coffee. "He's probably long escaped the perimeter," he says, reading my mind, then takes a sip. "If he caught a taxi, or took the train, he could be all the way to the Mall of America. Maybe even gotten a ride from some trucker." He points to a gas station a block from the Mall.

"Which means by now, he could be in Tennessee."

"Or Colorado, or Montana." Burke finishes off his coffee.

"Did we check the bus stations?"

"Yes. Scanned all the cameras, and talked with the employees on staff at the time. No one matching Fitzgerald's description came on the radar."

I walk over to the known associates board. Look it over. "And no one here has seen him?"

"Not for years."

Like I said, slippery.

"He'll make a mistake, Rem," Burke says, but his words do nothing to dent the roil in my gut.

My phone vibrates and I fish it out of my pocket. Eve.

"Hey babe, what's up?"

"I'm at the house, Rem. And besides it being dark and creepy, I'm not sure what you want. Clothes? Books?"

Deep sigh. "I have no idea."

"I'll be here for a while. Can you come by?"

"I don't know. I'm pretty tied up here—"

"Go," Burke says, and he's one to talk. He's supposed to be on paternity leave. But there's nothing worse than sitting at home when you want to be on the front lines. Shelby's five phone calls today have told me that much. "You can't do anything from here," he adds.

He's right. Burke is at the helm of the task force.

"I'll be there as soon as I can," I say.

"I was thinking I should get the baby clothes out of storage. You know, just in case the remodel takes longer."

I smile, glance at Burke, then turn away. "Yes, you should."

I know what you're thinking. It's high risk, Eve is older, but women have babies, even at this age. And I have a good feeling about this baby. Besides, fate owes me, don't you think? I pause.

"Everything is going to be okay," I say again, for both of us.

"Love you, Rem," she says and hangs up.

Love you, too.

"You all right?" Burke asks I pocket my phone.

I nod. "Let's just find Fitzgerald so I can get on with the rest of my life."

"I'm going to make more coffee," Burke says, and I leave him to that.

I have Danny's truck, and rain spits on the windshield as I pull onto the street, the sky an eerie green. Traffic is snarled—I'm caught in rush hour, and by the time I pull up to the house, it's over an hour later and dark outside. But Eve probably took a cab, and I think the electricity is off to the house, so I park at the curb and run through the downpour to the front porch.

Our poor house. With the tree gone, it looks like a giant thumb has pressed in the roof, one side of the porch sagging. The front door is ajar, so she must be here. I push it open and turn on my phone light. "Eve?"

No answer. I step inside. The place still smells soggy and mildewed. We'll have to replace everything. "Eve?"

Maybe she's upstairs, but our bedroom has been roped off— probably Sams' work. He's also put up plastic sheeting over the open edge of the room. I stand in the shadowy darkness and listen to the rain hit the plastic. It's almost enough to drown out the thump of my heartbeat.

Stop panicking, Rem. She's fine. But I dial her number anyway. It goes to voicemail.

I head back down the stairs, and it's in the landing that I hear a sound in the kitchen. A chair scraping back, maybe. "Eve?"

The family room is dark, and I work my way through it and stand at the door between the dining room and kitchen. More plastic covers the destroyed walls, the open roof. I flick my light around the room.

No Eve.

I turn back, to retrace my steps and that's when I see him sitting in my wife's rocking chair, the one she inherited from her grandmother.

He's simply rocking, a creak on the floor from his weight. I swallow, and the sound is deafening in my head.

"Hello, Detective."

I flash my light at him, just to make sure, and he puts up a hand, wincing. I hold it there. "How long have you been here, Leo?"

He puts his hand down, like he doesn't care about the light anymore, and looks at me, his gaze even. "Were you looking for someone else?"

Everything inside me goes cold.

"She's not here."

I don't react.

"I mean, she *was* here, but…she left."

"Where is she, Leo?"

He continues rocking. "She's very pretty. I can see why you married her. And smart. A crime scene investigator? I looked her up while I was waiting for you." He holds up a phone.

It looks like Eve's, with the Bones cover, from the television show, one of her favorites.

Maybe she's still in the house. I turn off the light, but as I do, I text 911 to Burke. Slip the phone into my pocket and hold up my hands. "Leo, this doesn't have to end badly—"

"Doesn't it?" He stops rocking. "You didn't have to come to Florida, did you? You could have left me alone. Believed me when I said I didn't hurt those girls."

"Did you hurt Eve?" My voice doesn't shake, but it wants to.

He lifts his shoulders. "Dunno yet."

I close my eyes. *Please, God.* Open them. "Just tell me where she is, and you walk away. Just disappear." I'm holding up my hands. "I won't come after you."

He shakes his head. "I think we're past that."

"We're not—"

"Johnny says we are!" He shouts it, a quick burst of heat and fury that grabs my bones and shakes hard.

Then he sucks in a breath, shaking his head, as if he's even scared himself. "Johnny says Eve knows too much. That she has to die. And Johnny knows what to do. He always knows."

"Leo—"

"And that you have to be stopped."

He gets to his feet.

My breath is in hitches. Worse, I'm not carrying.

I hold up my hands. "I'll stop, Leo, just—"

He rushes me.

Maybe I learned more than I thought from the MMA fighters in my gym, but I sidestep him, turn and pounce on him, slamming him into the floor. I try for a submission hold, but he's fast and he rolls, throwing me off.

When I crash into a table, a lamp takes the hit, shattering on the floor.

I stagger to my feet, but he's faster. He takes me down and sends a ringer into the side of my face. I see gray, but I've got him by the throat, and I pull him down and slam a left into his jaw.

He headbutts me and now I'm fighting blind, blood in my eyes, pain dissolving through my face. But I don't let him go.

I'm never letting him go.

He's my only connection to Eve. So I curl my legs around him and continue to beat his ear even as he does the same to me.

My head is ringing, and he's grunting. And then, behind the rush of pain and adrenaline, through the thunder and onslaught of rain, sirens pierce the night.

He hears it too, and pushes off me, finding his feet.

I do the same. "Tell me where she is."

"You're not taking me," he says, his eyes hot. Then he picks up my fireplace poker.

Aw. "Put it down, Leo—"

"I didn't kill those guys in the jail." He lunges at me, and I slap it away.

"Yeah, then who did?"

"Johnny."

Right. He lunges again, and I grab the poker and pull him in, slamming my elbow into his face. His nose explodes and now we're both bloody. He goes down and I pounce on him, and sure, he's bigger than me, but like I said, I'm not letting him go.

He's trying to pull me off, but I have him in a choke hold.

Somehow, he's grabbed the poker.

He slams it against my head, and the world turns white.

Next thing I know, I'm on the floor.

And Leo is on top of me, the poker against my neck.

Again, I'm drowning, the last of my air escaping my lungs.

I'm struggling, but with my head spinning, I got nothin'.

Leo's not moving, and another ringer to my jaw has me nearly out.

But I refuse to give up. I get my hand around a shard of the broken lamp.

I'm all about adrenaline. Instinct.

I swing the shard into the side of Leo's neck, deep.

He reels back, his hands going to his wound.

I've hit the carotid.

He falls back. Pulls the impalement from his neck, slaps his hands over the wound.

It clicks in, then.

I don't know where Eve is. No, no—

Rolling to my knees, I scramble over to him, put my hands over the gush of blood, trying to seal it up. "Leo, where is Eve!"

His face is whitening, and he's lost his anger.

He's afraid. I see it in his eyes, and now I am too. "Eve. Tell me where she is."

His mouth opens. Blood spittles out. "Johnny took her."

Oh, God. "Leo—where did you take her!"

Voices, and my front door bangs in. "Police!"

"Here—I'm here!" I shout. "Get a bus, now!"

"C'mon, Leo."

He looks at me, blinking, almost in disbelief. "Johnny did it. He takes what you love." His face crumples. "He takes *everything*."

What? "Where did he take her?"

Leo's eyes widen and he takes one last breath. "Home. He took her home." Then he's gone. I grab him by the shirt. "Leo, stay with me!"

Burke is on his knees next to me, reaching for the wound, trying to help. "What happened?"

Leo is unresponsive, his blood a lake on my wooden floor. Burke takes his pulse, puts his hand over his mouth. "He's gone, man."

"No, no—give him CPR."

"He's got no blood to circulate. It's done."

I stare at him, and slowly pull my hands away. They're shaking, and there's so much blood, from him, from me, the room is helter skelter. I sit back, trying to breathe. "Maybe it was a bluff.

Maybe she's okay. Maybe—"

"Who?" Burke asks.

I lean against the wall, just needing something to hold me up. I look at Burke. "Eve. He took Eve."

CHAPTER 19

"He said he took her home." I'm standing in the great room of Danny's house, the sky ravaging the yard, the lake violent as it throws itself on shore.

I'm drenched, bloody and injured and I don't care. Because Eve isn't here.

"Rembrandt, you look awful. You need to get that contusion looked at," Bets says, but I glance at Danny and see I have an ally.

He's nearly white with horror, especially after Burke has briefed him on what went down at the house.

"Bets," he says. "Let's give the guys room to think." Danny puts his arm around her. "Maybe make some coffee."

I know it's just so she'll have something to do because I'm not sticking around here long enough for a cup of coffee. And I'm not going to the hospital either.

The police searched my house—no sign of Eve. Not that I expected any, but it took up time while I gave my quick statement to Burke.

While I called Danny to see if Eve had indeed, come home.

I followed up his no with a look-see for myself, stymied.

The only home we've ever known is the one Leo died in.

Burke hands me a towel for my now swollen nose. It contains ice and I hold it there while I think. *He took her home.*

I look at Burke, then. He's as wrecked as I am, bloodied from both Leo and me, his eyes red, and I can tell he's worried.

Once upon a time, remember, he was married to Eve. And while they never went down that road in this lifetime, I know he loves her.

"What if he means *my* home," I say suddenly. "You know, because of the bodies."

Danny has come to join us, and now frowns. "What bodies?"

"We found five more Jackson killer bodies in Rembrandt's backyard a few days ago, all of them Jackson murders," Burke says.

"But I never lived there. It hasn't been my home since—"

"Since those bodies were found, about ten years after your brother went missing." Danny says. "Your parents moved to Florida."

I look at him. "What bodies?"

"It was the biggest news item in the decade. And it got picked up again when a body of another missing kid was found in the lake where your brother was, well..."

"Left. I get it."

Danny is thinking, and I can see the old cogs moving. "I remember that Booker was beside himself. He'd caught him dumping your brother's body. He'd been investigating five other murders, the boys' bodies still missing, and when this body was found, he was furious."

Five other kids. I look at him.

"The guy who killed your brother—Donald Simmons—was doing time in Stillwater, and we went to get him, and we took him to the lake. Then we drove the road where your brother was taken, trying to get him to confess to the other murders."

"Why," Bets says from behind us.

"Because serial murderers like to return to the place of the crime," I say quietly.

She looks a little horrified.

"What does this have to do with Rem?" Burke says, and I can tell he's getting impatient.

"You know that serial killers have groupies, right? Groupie boards? And Michelangelo Stone's case was the biggest to hit our state in years, and it got replayed in the press over and over. Maybe Fitzgerald was on one of those boards. Maybe he lifted Rem's address from there," Danny says.

"Maybe his dumping of the bodies had nothing to do with our fight in Montrose, and everything to do with a crazy memorial to the killer he admired."

Bets chimes in. "Like flowers in memorial at highway accidents."

"Get a squad out there," Danny says to Burke, but he's already on the phone.

And I'm headed to the door. But Danny grabs the keys off the counter. "I'm driving."

Burke has his squad car, but I hop in with Danny. He's out of the driveway before Burke leaves the house.

Never mind the speed limit.

I'm silent in the darkness.

"We'll find her," Danny says, and I glance over. His knuckles are nearly white on the steering wheel. I wish he'd added the word, *alive*.

The rain pelts the windshield, the wipers on full, a harsh rhythm as we fly past Excelsior, toward Waconia. The pavement is shiny and slick, but the truck is heavy and we flatten out as we leave the city limits.

It occurs to me, then, "Why was Booker on my brother's case? It's outside the Minneapolis city limits." I don't know why this question never hit me before.

"It's because the first victim was in the city limits, a boy about ten. Simmons drove an ice-cream truck, and would target kids, then follow them, and kidnap them—you don't want to know this."

I probably don't, but I've read enough of my brother's case to understand the rest. "I don't remember an ice-cream truck the day Mickey went missing."

"He'd taken the decals off his van, but he'd been in town earlier that day. That's how Booker connected him."

Right. What Danny doesn't know of course, is that I have no recollection of any of this.

"Did he ever confess to the other murders?"

Danny nods. "Yes. I thought you knew all this."

I say nothing. "Hurry, Danny."

He cuts west on 41, then hits Highway 5 and I'm counting the miles.

We pass Lake Auburn and the last development and then hit the countryside, farmland, occasional homes, open fields, barns.

A crackle of lightning fractures the sky, followed by the low roll of thunder. The swift and brutal memory of Eve in my arms as we huddle under the table hits my chest and I just barely keep from crying out.

Please. God.

It's more of a primal instinct than a real prayer, any faith I had scrubbed out of me with my brother's death. But I'm desperate.

I see the lights circling, turning the night blood red as we approach my house. The sky crackles again, and I spot the barn, the old house, a broken windmill, the blades stripped off.

Danny slows, and pulls in.

There are only two cars here, two men out with flashlights. One is staring through our sagging front door. The other is standing near the yellow tape in the field, still a working crime scene.

I get out, oblivious of the rain and run up the porch, into the house.

The officer turns and I say, "Chief Stone," and move past him. "Eve?" I check the kitchen, then our small family room, my father's empty den, then run upstairs.

I stand in my childhood bedroom, looking down, watching as lights splash through the yard. More cops arriving.

She's not in the bathroom, or my parents' room or the closet. Or, even, Mickey's room. The memory of him catches me as I poke my head in. *Hey Rem, can I go with you to the lake?*

I can't be here.

Please, let this not be the place my wife dies, too.

Downstairs, I hear voices, and I find Burke talking with the first cop. "She's not here."

"We've got guys in the field, but we don't see anything fresh."

My stomach drops. *Fresh.*

"Like a *grave*? What do you think—that he killed her and *buried* her? Oh man—" I push past him, out to the porch, and then to the yard and grab my knees, just trying to breathe.

Lightning again, and it illuminates the barn, the open door, shuddering in the breeze. Darkness lies inside.

I let out a breath, and head toward it.

"Rem, wait!" Burke is behind me, but I ignore him. Maybe deep in my bones I know, already.

Or maybe it's just my fear. I push the barn door aside, and it screams on its old hinges. The place smells of oil and grease and dirt and a thousand hours with my father fixing my old Porsche, my first real love.

He takes what you love.

I stand in the middle of the barn, the rain pounding on the slats of the roof. "Eve." It's not a shout, just a breath.

The lightning flashes again—the storm is roiling up—and in the flicker of light, I see it.

Something shiny and gold in the wooden floor and packed dirt.

I walk over and pick it up.

Her necklace, the one with the heart charm. The one her father gave her for her sixteenth birthday. I close it in my palm.

Eve.

"Rem?"

"I need a light," I say to Burke, and he hands me a flashlight. I take it, my hand shaking because even in the darkness, I can see signs of a struggle. The dirt kicked up, the mud on the floor.

Footprints.

"Rem—" Burke reaches out to me, but I push him away and follow the steps.

The barn used to house our few dairy cows, a horse, a pen of goats.

Stalls that my father eventually filled with auto parts.

"Rembrandt—"

"Shut up!" I reach the stall.

Hands are on me, grabbing my arms, but I break away, fall to my knees and crawl over to her.

She's laying with her back to me, her beautiful red hair grimy and wet, tangled. Her shirt is ripped in back, as if he had a hold of her and yet she got away.

"Eve?" I reach out to her, and Burke has stopped trying to

intervene. Her body is limp, and I roll her over.

I know bodies after the life has left them, the feel of them, boneless yet unbearably heavy, their spirit departed.

Eve's body is leaden.

Her face is ashen, bruising on her neck, and her eyes are puffy and bruised.

Closed.

Oh. God.

"Eve," I say, and I can feel myself fracturing. Strange, I've delivered terrible news to dozens, maybe a hundred people in my career, and I've never really understood how the realization of our news travels over them.

See, in my original life, my true life, we never truly embraced Mickey's death. And Ashley, well I still haven't accepted it, if I'm honest.

I pull Eve to myself, just trying to hold on. And when I pull the twenty-dollar bill from her staged, frozen grip, I know it's no use.

Eve is gone.

And so am I.

CHAPTER 20

They say I picked her up, and clung to her, held her in my arms, tried to breathe life into her. They say I guarded her body, even after the EMTs showed up, refusing to hand her over. They say Burke and Danny, who were also wrecked, had to wrestle her away from me.

They say I didn't speak for hours, even after they took me to the hospital to check my head. I had a concussion. I didn't notice, not with my world already fractured.

They say I'll be okay, someday.

They don't know me.

He takes everything.

Leo's words are an anvil in my head as I stand at the window, staring out into the yard. It's still raining.

Behind me in the kitchen, Bets is busy, cleaning up after the funeral reception. It's what she does, tragedy becoming a task she can manage with food preparation, funeral arrangements and thank you cards.

Burke and Shelby are still here. Shelby is trying to figure out if she should appoint a new chief. Maybe Burke.

I've destroyed his plans to retire. Fate, at work, course correcting, again.

Danny is helpless, frustrated, and doesn't know what to say to me after he found me on the dock last night, in the rain, staring down at the murky lake water.

He didn't say what he was thinking, what I was thinking.

This is not my life.

Eve doesn't have a gravestone yet, but we buried her beside Ashley. I stood at the edge of the draped hole—they make it look like it isn't a cement box they're going to seal her in—and stared at Ashley's white stone.

Her handprint is crafted into it, tiny, brave, permanent.

I wanted to press my own into it, remind myself that she was real. But I didn't.

Because it can't be real.

"Rembrandt?" It's Frankie. I can't look at her. "Is there anything I can do?"

"No." I say. "But thanks."

She doesn't leave though, just standing there beside me. And maybe there's a cruel streak in me because I say, straight out, no emotion. "She was pregnant."

Frankie sucks in her breath. "Oh, Rem."

I lift a shoulder.

And before you think I'm too nonchalant, that I don't care, you know what I'm thinking, don't you? I'm guessing you're thinking the same thing.

I have a plan. Only the fact that I was under heavy painkillers, and generally supervised by Danny, has slowed me down. I have the watch. And I'm going back.

I've figured out when, too.

I'll go back to the day of Booker's death. I'll save him, and me, and keep Danny from becoming chief. I'll propose to Eve and *keep* proposing until she says yes. Then I'll track down Leo Fitzgerald.

And I will kill him.

I know what you're going to say, but I don't have a choice.

He's going to kill forty-three women, two cops, my wife and my daughter. What would you do?

The world is a better place without Leo Fitzgerald and his crazy alter-ego Johnny.

This is justice. And yes, Eve is in my head, telling me I'm better than this, but I don't think I am.

In fact, I know I'm not. Eve made me better.

And Eve isn't here.

"I don't know why this terrible thing has happened," Frankie says softly. Her hand is on my arm. "But I do know that God has a plan."

I give her a look. "Really?"

"C'mon, Frankie, I'll take you home," Zeke says. He holds out his hand, and I shake it. "Call us if you need anything."

Frankie hugs me, gently. "I'm so sorry, Rem. But yes, really."

I nod, give her a small smile. I know they'd all like it if I pretended to be okay, so I'll try to.

At least for the next hour.

But what kind of plan is this, God? God has a plan? I hate those words. And most of what the pastor said at the service about eternity and hope and heaven.

Any hope I have I hold in my hands.

Shelby and Burke say goodbye too, and I press my hand on Daphne's head, lean down and kiss it. I really hope I don't steal this from them.

They leave and Bets is still cleaning, and Danny has gone to his office. Eve's brothers are all in town, Lucas and his family from

Chicago, and Jake, from his posting in the Navy. They're staying with Sams and Asher.

I'm still soggy from the funeral, probably down to my soul, but I'm ready. "Bets," I say, walking over to her. She's been crying, her eyes puffy, but Bets is every bit as strong as her daughter was. "Thank you for everything you did for me—us—today."

She looks up at me, gives me a sad smile and touches my hand. "Rembrandt, you are a son to us. That hasn't changed."

My throat tightens and I nod. I hope I still am in the future. I pull off my tie as I head upstairs.

Every time I jump, I return back in the same place, so I've figured it out. I'll drive to the house, and jump there, and if all goes well, our house will be intact and Eve will be waiting for me.

And maybe—Oh, God, please—Ashley.

I can see it, can't you?

I throw the tie on the bed and go over to the cold case files. From past jumps, I have to have the case in my hand, or near it, I think. And be wearing the watch.

I rifle through the case files and find Booker's shooting. Before Booker was shot, the perp killed the clerk, so I'll have a few minutes to save Booker.

This is going to work. It has to work.

I tuck the file under my arm, grab the gift bag, still on the nightstand, and head outside to Danny's truck, nabbing the keys off the ring by the door as I leave.

I suppose I should ask if I can borrow his ride, but what does it matter? If it works I'm going to be gone anyway.

The house is still untouched. I stand in the rain imagining Eve sitting on the porch, tying her shoes before a run. Ashley drawing in chalk on the front walk. Me, the light on in the den window, typing away in my fruitless efforts to be a novelist.

I will get my life back.

The door is unlocked, and I push my way inside, to the smell of creosote and wet wood and sit on the stairs. Put the file on my lap.

Then I open the bag and pull out the box. It's a watch box, inlaid with wood and marble—fancy. But maybe the right place for Booker to store something so precious, an ancient watch that can help a guy change time.

Booker is in my head. *Here are the rules. The biggest one, the one that is never, ever to be broken…Don't change the past.*

Whatever.

As I open the watch case, he's still talking. *The watch was created to find answers, bring closure. To solve cases. And keep people from suffering.*

And I'm suffering.

I open the watch box.

My heart rate spikes. What—?

It's not the watch. I mean, it's a watch—from when he became police chief. It's a nice watch, a Rolex, of course. It's gold and looks as expensive as I'm sure it is.

But it's not our watch. My watch. *The* watch.

I stare at it, a band circling my chest. Panic claws the insides of my skull, leaving lines.

Maybe he was buried with it. Frankie's words zero back to me.

Frankie. Maybe she knows where it is. I just didn't describe it well enough. Of course she'd think of this watch, right?

I pull out my cell phone and scroll down. Frankie isn't in my contacts. But Zeke is.

And he's taking her home. I pull his name up, dial and steady my voice as he picks up.

"Rem?"

"Zeke, hey," I say. "I have to talk to Frankie—"

"Sure, I'll put her on."

"No!" I take a breath. "I mean, face to face. Can I come over?"

A pause. "Sure. I guess."

"Where are you?"

"I'm at Frankie's place."

I make a face and then, what do I have to lose? "Can you text me her address? I don't remember it."

"Yeah." There's no suspicion in his voice.

I hang up, and by the time I'm in the truck, the text comes in. She's on Hopkins street, just down the road.

The rain has slowed to a miserable drizzle. Her house is a tiny gray bungalow with the garage off the alley. I park at the curb and head to the front door.

Hit the doorbell.

The light turns on and Frankie opens the door. I'm standing out of the rain, under a small awning. She's wearing a pair of yoga pants, a T-shirt, and slippers. Her hair is down, and her eyes are red. She's been crying.

"Rem. Do you want to come in?"

I shake my head. "Frankie, I need Booker's watch."

She frowns. "But I gave you his watch—"

"Not the *right* watch!" Oh. I didn't mean to yell, I don't think. She recoils and Zeke appears at the door.

"Rem, are you okay?"

I'm shivering now, and I shove my shaking hands into my pockets. "Yes. No." I look at them. "Sorry." They just stare at me. "Listen. Booker used to have this watch. It was old. Very old. It had a worn leather band, and an open face, so you could see the gears, and it didn't work."

She shakes her head.

"He wore it *every single day*. You have to remember it!"

"Rem," Zeke says, and now he steps in front of her. "You're sorta freaking out here. Take a breath."

"Why would he wear it if it didn't work?" Frankie says, pushing Zeke back.

"Because—it—it *does* work. And I need it." And I might be crying a little, gimme a break, I can't stop. "I need it, Frankie. I have to have that watch."

I take a step forward and lift my hand, as if to grab her wrist, but Zeke steps in front of her. "Listen, Rem. She doesn't have it, okay? And you're scaring her."

Maybe I am, because her eyes are wide, and she's backed away.

"Frankie, I'm sorry, but I have to have that watch." And now I can't breathe. I bend over, taking in heavy gulps.

"Hey, why don't you come in," Zeke says. "Or, let me drive you home."

"No!" I stand up, still breathing hard. "I—no. I'm fine." I turn and stalk back out to the truck.

Maybe he was buried with it.

I saw Frankie wander off today, stand over a grave. It might have been her mother's.

But it might have also been Booker's.

I head back to the Mulligans.

It has to be done.

I find a shovel in the garage, throw it in the back of the truck and pull out.

It's the only way.

Eve is buried in a cemetery not five minutes from her parents' home, in a family section. It's next to an elementary school, and at the edge of a park, and I suppose the fact that she might hear children playing should comfort me.

Not in the least.

I pull up, and the chain link gate is closed, the place cordoned off by fencing.

Not a problem. I throw the shovel over and leap the fence, still in my dress pants and shoes. The ground is soggy, muddy, so it'll be soft. Good for digging.

That's just where I'm at.

Her grave is easy to find. They've closed up the dirt, but a green blanket lays over the mound. I don't even pause as I walk by.

This is not my world.

I stalk over to where I saw Frankie wander, and read the gravestones, shining my phone light on each one.

Booker's is a black marble stone, stately and fierce, but I would have expected something a little more rough-hewn. Something made of granite, maybe, chiseled out with a pick.

But at least he's here.

I set my shovel in the ground, and it gives.

Stop. I know this is a crime. But…

It might be buried with him.

I start digging. The ground is dense, heavy and impossible. But I move the dirt, digging down, then across, then down again. I slip, getting into the hole, and my entire body is muddy. My shirt, my pants.

My face.

The rain and mud mixes with tears that won't stop coming. I just keep digging.

It's an hour, maybe more, by the time I hit something. My shovel pings, the sound of it dull in the night and rain, which has died to a fine mist.

I hit it again. And then I realize.

Cement.

Of course. His casket is encased in cement. I close my eyes. And then, I release a sound that frightens even me. It's soul wrenching and raw and I heave the shovel out of the hole and fall to my knees in the grave.

"You did this! You did this, you stupid…" I have words, but they aren't enough, and all I can do is lean over, my forehead to the cement, my hands over my head, and weep.

I wish this damn watch had never come to me. That I didn't let my regrets tell me how to live my life.

That I chose happiness instead of the what-ifs.

I was wrong. There *are* happy endings.

I had one.

"Oh wow—Rembrandt!" The words come from above, and I'm too wrecked to be ashamed that Zeke and Frankie have found me in a muddy hole, kneeling on the grave of a man who destroyed my life.

I sit up, lifting my face to the drizzle.

"What are you doing?"

I shrug. "Nothing. I'm doing nothing." My voice is eerily hollow.

Zeke holds an umbrella over Frankie, who is wearing a slicker. But, she's holding a box. "I found this."

I glance at it, at Zeke, and then back to her. "What is it?"

"Come out of there," Zeke says.

I almost don't take his hand as he reaches down. But I finally let him pull me from the grave.

Frankie is standing a few paces back, surveying the destruction. "I'm sorry, Rembrandt. I didn't understand…I would have—"

"Give him the box, Frankie," Zeke says.

It's a file box, and she sets it down in front of me. "They sent this over about a year after his death. My mom put it in the closet

211

and after she died, I just…I just moved it with my things. I didn't realize that…"

I'm staring at her. "What?"

"It's his things. From the day he died. The police had them for evidence for a while. But they finally released them to my mom."

I'm still sorting out her words as I crouch and lift the cover from the box. Inside, in baggies, are his clothes. His pants, still blood stained, his shirt, also stained. His badge is in another bag, his wallet in yet another.

And in yet another, way on the bottom, under his shoes, a tiny bag that holds a watch with an old leather band. I pull it out.

Swallow.

"Is that it?" Frankie says, also crouching. She reaches for it, and I look at her. "I'll give it back."

My hand trembles as I drop it into hers. She rubs her thumb over the face, through the plastic. "It is old."

"I don't get it, Rem," Zeke says slowly. "Why do you need this watch?" He's looking at the desecration of the grave, then at me. And I have a lot of explaining to do.

And you know, I don't care. I'm tired. Tired of the lies and of dodging the truth. I'm just…tired. "It's a time-travel watch. It lets the wearer travel in time, solve cold cases—"

"Fix the past," Frankie says. She doesn't look at me like I'm crazy. Just takes a breath and nods.

Like she *knows*. Or at least, isn't completely wigged out by this idea. She hands me back the watch. "Have you…used it before?"

That is not the question I expected. I take a breath, and whisper, "Yes."

Glance at Zeke. He's considering my words, a strange expression on his face. "You've changed the past."

I nod.

"Which changes the future," Frankie says. "You can stop Eve from getting murdered."

I hope so. Again, I nod.

Zeke is looking so hard at me, it feels like he might be looking through me. Finally, "How does it work?"

"Not now, Zeke," Frankie says, her hand on his arm.

He takes a breath. Nods. "Will we know?"

I think there's more to his question, fears about him and Frankie, and maybe even his life.

"No," I say. "But I already…well, if all goes well, then maybe, Frankie, you don't grow up without your father."

She nods slowly and gets up. "Are you going now?"

I blow out a breath. Look at the grave. "Yeah. Soon."

"Get out of here," Zeke says. "Before someone shows up and sees the mess you made." He offers a tiny grin. Something releases inside of me, as if suddenly I have partners, or at least friends.

I look at Frankie. "Thank you."

She's holding Zeke's hand. "Go save my dad."

I start to walk, then sprint in the slippery grass, back to the truck. Get inside. I know I should probably go somewhere…safe. But then again, who knows where that is, really, anymore. And I can't wait. With shaking hands, I open the baggie and pull out the watch.

The band is worn and soft, and I put it on, tighten it down. It's an old friend.

Please, please work.

I won't go for long. Just to save Booker, propose to Eve. Maybe take down a tree.

And kill Leo Fitzgerald.

And then I'll come back to a life I can live with.

My chest is tight, and I'm blowing out hard against a surge of panic, maybe anticipation.

I need this to work more than I need my heart to beat.

I pick up the file, still on the seat.

Then I wind the watch, close my eyes and pray.

The epic series continues with Rembrandt Stone in two months. Check out a sneak peek of book five. Join us in October for the next installment.

THE TRUE LIES OF REMBRANDT STONE

BLOOD FROM A STONE

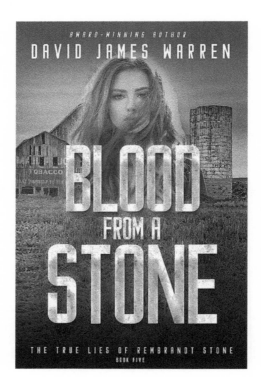

BLOOD FROM A STONE
SNEAK PEAK

This is not my world.

Not my life.

Not my time.

Sure, it resembles a life I knew—from the snow piled up along the blackened, salted streets, the icy wind buffeting the frosty diner window, to the sound of Celine Dion singing how her heart will gone on, and even the smell of oil in the fryers of the late-night diner. It could be any one of the diners I used to frequent in downtown Minneapolis after a long day of investigations.

But this is not my life.

My life is twenty years in the future, and right now, if fate were kind, or even fair, I would be reading Llama, Llama, Red Pajama to my seven year old blonde cherub as she clutches a ratty one-eyed bear named Gomer and tells me to slow down, to read it again.

My gorgeous wife, Eve would be standing in the doorway, of our partially remodeled craftsman located in a suburb of uptown. Or maybe she'd be across the hall in our king bed, bundled up in her wool socks and thick bathrobe, her reading glasses down on her nose, deep in the latest issue of the Journal for Forensic Scientists.

Downstairs, the light in my den would be on, the cursor at my computer blinking, waiting for me to continue my half-finished novel.

And I would be happy. Until now, I wouldn't realize how happy, but as I sit here, I know.

I had a happy ending.

This is not it. But this time around, if I'm smart, I'll win.

I must win.

To time travelers, until you've been someplace for a long time, traveling feels like a game. We jump into the moment, armed with knowledge we shouldn't possess, the older and wiser versions of ourselves, with the goal of rewriting our lives, this time for the better.

For us, the game isn't win or lose, but rather, scored on the what-ifs that we grab, the shoulda's we accomplish. And, all the while, in the back of our minds, if we make a wrong move, we're buoyed by the surety it can be reset.

It's taken me four rounds, but this time I know.

This is not a game.

Time is playing for keeps and there's no reset if I fail.

But don't worry—this time, I will not be bested.

I swear it on my life.

I keep that information tucked inside, my countenance cool, as I sit in a booth, across from a man long since dead, but now very much alive, Minneapolis Police Chief John Booker. My mentor, friend and the man who will save my life in roughly six minutes and forty-two seconds.

In Jin's Liquors, the store next door, right now, a robbery is going down, and if we don't leave now, the owner will be shot in the chest by a Colt. .38. He'll bleed out in less than five minutes, but before collapsing, he'll pull his alarm.

And because Booker and I are next door, we'll respond.

I should probably mention that I'm a Homicide Investigator with the Minneapolis Police department. When I left, I was also the interim Police Chief, so at this point I'm pretty good at this game.

I'll go in first, breaking through the front doors, and see the downed owner. Going immediately to his aid, I won't see the perp coming out of the back room hauling the contents of the safe. I also won't see him aim his gun at me and pull the trigger.

I especially won't see Booker push me away, behind a display of Seagram's wine coolers.

The gunshot will hit the Chief.

He'll die next to the owner within the next two minutes, leaving a legacy of heroism, and taking with him a slew of questions I now need answers to.

But we'll get to those.

Because this time, he will live. I've studied every detail of this scene.

I know how to win.

"So, tell me, Rem, how's she doing?"

We're talking about my current partner, rookie investigator Shelby Ruthers. In my time, she's the Minneapolis Police Chief.

Here, I'm tasked with training her. And apparently, Booker is keenly interested in her progress.

At least, I think that's why we're sitting in a diner on a Friday night at 10 p.m. eating pie.

Maybe he has something else on his mind—I don't know. I've never lived this rewrite of time before.

The details of his death I learned from his jacket, the one included in my stack of cold case files, his killer never apprehended.

But that file is never going to be made.

Like I said, things will go down differently this time.

This time, I'll get there early. And maybe I won't be able to save the life of the owner, but John Booker will not die.

Neither will I.

The perp will get away, at least for the next forty-eight hours. I know what you're thinking, but he will go down for his crimes. Just not yet.

Before then I have to bring another murderer to justice.

The man who killed my wife.

It's a long story, so wait for it. Because, right now, I just need to answer Booker, then figure out how to get next door before the alarm sounds.

Before history repeats itself.

"She's nailing it," I say to his question about Shelby and take a sip of coffee. I like this place—it's a tucked away diner in a strip mall near Chicago avenue and 36th just outside of downtown Minneapolis. They serve killer pies, and sometimes Booker and I sneak away for the house special—Grandma Lou's lemon angel chiffon.

The place is unimpressive—a long counter display that shows the various pies, a few drugstore stools mounted in front of the Formica counter, retro tables with vinyl yellow chairs and cafe curtains at the window.

But the pie—oh, I'd forgotten how the lemon tart dissolves in your mouth with just the right balance of salty, lard-based crust, and a hint of fluffy meringue. It's almost enough to distract me.

Not quite. I have an eye on the parking lot, looking for movement. Last time, the perp escaped out the back, and I've already spotted a door to the back of the diner.

But, like I said, I don't want to catch the shooter. Not yet. He's not why I'm here. Just a by-product, collateral justice, as it were.

But the moment he's caught is the moment this ride through time ends.

And I've got stuff to do, places to be before I close the books on this jump.

"That's good," Booker says, still talking about Shelby, "because Danny hired her on your recommendation. But we need to get her trained because Burke is finished with his assignment with Danny's task force, now that Hassan Abdilhali is dead. His gang is in disarray, and the Minneapolis drug trade is ripe for a new regime."

"So, Burke is looking for a new partner?" I take another bite of pie—my last one, because I've gotta figure out how to leave in about forty seconds.

Booker gives me a wry grin. He's always seemed a man from a different time, as if he walked straight from the pages of Lonesome Dove, fresh from leading a posse, a wizened look of battle in his eyes. He is tall, with slightly graying hair, and speaks with a low baritone, his words slow, thoughtful. But his dark brown eyes are always studying, weighing.

I wonder if I measure up.

"Burke will always be your partner, Rem. You know that." Booker takes a sip of his coffee.

It's then I notice he's wearing a wedding ring, and my mind flips back to the woman I met back in my real time, a reporter named Frankie.

The daughter Booker never had in our original timeline.

So, he's married, although if my memory of Frankie's story is correct, he and her mother are separated.

Frankie will lose her father tonight if my rewrite doesn't take.

I glance out the window, toward the street and frown. A ruse, but Booker notices. "What?"

"Thought I saw something…" I get up, move toward the door, and he follows.

"What did you see?"

"Isn't the liquor store closed?" I push out into the night, knowing he'll follow.

Around the force, I'm known for my hunches. You know by now what they are—foreknowledge. And maybe Booker knows it too. But he's on my tail because I'm also a cop and I see things that shouldn't be.

It's late January, and my breath fogs the air, the chill finding my nose, slithering down my neck. The fresh snowfall is piled up around the perimeter of the lot, and an icy layer of danger coats the steps and sidewalks.

Streetlights shine against the dark windows of the liquor store, but as we walk down the sidewalk, a light flashes in the back.

Cheater, you say, but gimmie a break, I need an edge if I hope to pull this off.

We pause outside the window, and it's then the gunshot barks.

No alarm, not yet, and I hoof it down to the door. It's locked, the closed sign on it, but a glance inside shows the owner down, writhing and bleeding out.

He might live if we can get to him. In my previous go-round, according to the file, I kicked the door in.

This time I say, "Call it in!" Then take off for the back of the building.

The back door is open, and if I stage this right, no one will die.

I figure, if Booker can't get inside, he can't get shot, right?

Including me.

I spot a car idling in the back. It's a Toyota Supra, a hotrod wanna be, but it has nothing on my Porsche, bless her, now a sooty shell back in my time. I snapshot the license plate in my mind and move toward the door.

It's unlocked.

My plan is simple. Slip inside, making enough noise that the perp hears me and flees. And I'll let him go, for now. I'll pull the owner behind the counter—maybe save his life—and only after the perp has escaped will I unlock the front door.

And Booker will live.

One game point for Rembrandt Stone.

I steal in and spot a light on in the back office, a lamp light. The alarm is still sounding, so it might mask my noise, but even so, I hustle to the front of the building, grabbing a towel off a mop and rack sitting near the door.

The owner is groaning, laying near the front checkout desk and I kneel before him. He's a middle-aged Korean man, and the shot has hit him in his upper right side. "Hang in there," I say as I shove the towel against his wound.

He grabs my wrist, and it's stronger than I would imagine. "Help."

The words still me because he's a ghost from the grave.

"Jin-Sun…my…daughter…"

My eyes widen because I don't remember a daughter in the report.

"Where?"

"In…office…

I bite back a word, then swallow and nod.

And that's when I hear the voice that chills me through. "Rem. We have backup coming."

Booker has come in the front. I don't know if he's broken the lock, or simply slammed through the glass, but he now stands between me and the perp, who, by my estimation, is still emptying the safe.

With Jin-Sun hiding nearby.

And now the game has changed.

Booker is the target. And time is trying to win.

I can almost hear the laughter.

I figure one of two things could happen.

Booker will still get shot. And Frankie will grow up without her father. And the recent past will spool out like it did before—with Danny Mulligan becoming Police Chief, and his daughter, Eve, who I love, moving to Florida, out of his protective reach.

I will lose her all over again to a Miami cop named Val.

And Val will lead us to a serial killer who takes her life.

And sure, there are thousands of ways that might change, but with each variation, each rewrite, my life veers even further off course. Brings me back to another world that has been rewritten into another unlivable version of the life I should have.

No. Not this time.

This time, everything will be different.

Of course, there is option two, where Booker will hear—and catch the perp—before he gets off his lethal shot. Maybe even kill him.

Which means this cold case is solved.

I will then immediately return to the dismal future I left, with me sitting in the rain outside the graveyard where my daughter and my wife are buried.

If that happens, I won't have time to track down Leo Fitzgerald, the serial killer who, in my time, has murdered thirty-eight women, (including my daughter.) I won't have time to propose to Eve, and keep her from moving to Florida. I won't even have time to chop down the massive elm tree that will someday take out the craftsman home Eve and I love.

I know this is not about a tree, but as long as I'm counting my losses…

Thankfully, fate and I have been in the ring together before. It tried to steal my wife from me, three different ways.

Stole my partner from me.

Killed Booker in every timeline so far.

And swept my daughter and her memory from the face of the earth.

But what fate has forgotten is that I don't know what's good for me. And I'll keep swinging no matter how many times I get knocked flat.

I possess all the cheats.

And, I have nothing left to lose.

"Get down!" I get up, draw my weapon and point to the back—the wall, really, and pull off a shot. Booker turns, as if following my actions and that's when I dive at him.

It happens fast, so fast that Booker can't have noticed that indeed, no one stands in the back to take him out.

Yet.

We land in a painful tangle behind the display of Seagrams wine cooler, which crash around us in a splatter of glass and sticky, sweet alcohol.

A shot fires behind me. The front glass doors shatter.

I scramble off Booker and glance in the back.

The perp bursts through the door, into the night.

Yes!

I'm instantly on my feet and running hard to the door in false pursuit.

The getaway car has taken off, the taillights fading as it rounds the end of the strip mall, into the night.

Muffled sobbing, a hiccup of sound emerges from the office and I fear what I'll find.

The desk lamp splashes wan light into the room. A floor safe is open, the contents—mostly paper—spilled onto the floor.

The sounds come from under the desk. I walk over, then crouch and finally hit my hands and knees. "Jin-Sun?"

She's young—maybe nine years old, with big brown eyes and dark hair, She's sitting with her knees pulled to her chest, making herself small.

"You're safe." I keep my voice soft, gentle, a remnant of time when I was a father to a seven-year-old daughter. My throat thickens at the flash of memory, my Ashley sitting on her bed, her blue eyes thick with tears as she implores me to find Gomer, a silly bear I gave her for her fourth birthday. But daddy, you're a detective. You're supposed to find things.

I am, honey. And I'm going to find you, I promise.

I hold out my hand to Jin-Sun. "Come out. No one will hurt you."

She stares at my offering, and then places her hand in mine. It's soft, but she hangs on and I pull her out of the darkness. She stands before me, and then, throws her arms around me.

My breath rushes out of me and I can't help but wrap an arm around her, bracing myself with the other hand on the desk. "Everything is going to be okay," I whisper, and the words sink into me.

It's the last thing I said to Eve, right before Leo Fitzgerald kidnapped her and killed her.

I close my eyes, but the memory burns through me.

Eve, lying in my family's barn, her body gray and lifeless, a twenty-dollar bill—the calling card of the Jackson killer—in her grip.

Forcing the image away, I stand up and take Jin-Sun's hand. Sirens scream through the air, and as we walk out of the office, I see

Booker letting EMTs inside.

Jin-Sun squeezes my hand as they run up to her father, un-moving on the floor. I crouch next to her. "Honey, don't be afraid. They're going to help your daddy."

She looks at me though, with those big brown eyes and nods. "I'm not afraid."

"You're not?"

She shakes her head. "I prayed while I was hiding, and God sent you."

I have nothing.

I don't know why, but I can't help but feel that fate has won, again.

And I wonder who, really, is doing the cheating.

MEET
DAVID JAMES WARREN

Susan May Warren is the USA Today bestselling, Christy and RITA award–winning author of more than eighty novels whose compelling plots and unforgettable characters have won acclaim with readers and reviewers alike. The mother of four grown children, and married to her real-life hero for over 30 years, she loves travelling and telling stories about life, adventure and faith.

For exciting updates on her new releases, previous books, and more, visit her website at www.susanmaywarren.com.

James L. Rubart is 28 years old, but lives trapped inside an older man's body. He's the best-selling, Christy Hall of Fame author of ten novels and loves to send readers on mind-bending journeys they'll remember months after they finish one of his stories. He's dad to the two most outstanding sons on the planet and lives with his amazing wife on a small lake in eastern Washington.

More at www.jameslrubart.com

David Curtis Warren is making his literary debut in these novels, and he's never been more excited. He looks forward to creating more riveting stories with Susie and Jim, as well as on his own. He's grateful for his co-writers, family, and faith, buoying him during the pandemic of 2020-21, and this writing and publishing process.

CPSIA information can be obtained
at www.ICGtesting.com
Printed in the USA
LVHW020818271021
701667LV00004BA/533